TRANQUILLE DARK

A Blue in Kamloops Novel

By Alex McGilvery

Tranquille Dark

by Alex McGilvery

ISBN 978-1-989092-32-3

CELTICFROG PUBLISHING

CHAPTER 1
Thursday, April 25

The fight started between two young punks as Blue walked south on Tranquille toward the Duchess. The younger one, hardly more than a kid, quivered in rage as the other poked his chest. Whatever he was saying, the kid didn't like it. He spun away and stomped in Blue's direction.

The kid wasn't quite yelling—mostly swear words, as if they were the only thing to come to mind while he was angry. As he passed, he sent a punch at Blue's face. The would-be gang-banger's fist thudded against Blue's arms. The leather jacket absorbed most of the force. Undeterred, the kid kept swinging.

His face showed his frustration as his friends called out a mix of encouragement and mockery. His dirty blond hair straggled past his shoulders, partially hiding an unfinished tattoo. The guy this kid really wanted to beat up leaned against the wall of the Duchess, smoking and laughing. He tossed the cigarette on the ground and sauntered away.

"Hey, kid." Blue lowered his arms slightly to catch the young punk's eye. "Can we finish this up? I'd like to get a coffee to warm up."

"Shut up, old man." The kid swung hard. Blue stepped to the side and let it pass over his shoulder. "No homeless freak is going to make a fool of me."

Not like you need help with that.

The kid's friends were getting bored. They wanted to see blood, maybe land a few kicks of their own. If they

1

swarmed him, it would be trouble. Blue already struggled to keep his beast on its leash.

The kid pulled a knife. It snicked open—a gas station karambit, cheap steel, crap quality, but it could still kill.

"Hank..." one of the hangers-on called out uncertainly, but another punched his arm with a warning glare, then stared at Blue avidly waiting for blood.

Blue danced out of range and put a suitably nervous expression on his face. As he'd hoped when he saw the knife, Hank rushed in slashing wildly. He had no idea how to use the blade.

Blue caught Hank's arm and turned his hand to apply pressure to Hank's wrist. To the bystanders, it would look like he was desperately holding off the kid's attack. Hank's wide eyes showed the pain had cut through the anger.

"Listen, Hank." Blue spoke softly so only Hank would hear him. "You've proved yourself to be tough. Say something nasty and threaten to really cut me next time, then walk away laughing."

"And if I don't?" Hank's eyes hardened. Blue increased the pressure on the arm.

"I break your arm and you look like an idiot who can't take an old man." He met Hank's eyes and let him glimpse the beast hiding behind them.

"Next time, I'll gut you for real," Hank shouted before stepping back. Blue released him, ready for another attack, but Hank spun away, replacing the knife in his back pocket. "I don't want the cops after me for some worthless bum."

Blue sighed and waited until the group had walked away north toward Tim Horton's, forcing anyone in their path to jump aside. He'd get his coffee at Mac's today. Clenching and releasing his hands loosened the tension in his arms.

Damn, but I could use a drink. But when in the past two years had Blue *not* needed a drink? Caffeine would have to do.

"Blue?" A tentative voice caught his attention, and he looked around. A woman, younger than him, but looking older chewed her lip.

He softened his gaze and waited. She didn't need the spillover from the fight. While he waited for her to continue talking, he categorized her. He didn't smell any booze, but her hands twitched, and she was too thin. She'd washed her long black hair in the last day, so she had a place off the street, but no money for food or laundry.

"Rooster's missing." She stuffed her hands in the pocket of her bedraggled puffer jacket. He doubted she could fit so much as a cigarette paper in her jean's pocket. They were as tight as Hank's had been loose.

"Again?" Blue rolled his eyes. Rooster was missing more than he was around.

"We got a room at the Alpine, but it's the end of the month and he's the one pays the rent."

"Right." Blue stared into space for a moment, counting in his head. "It's the twenty-fifth today?"

"Yeah." She looked down. "I can't pay it myself. I talked to the others." Her face reddened, and she ducked her head. "None of them've heard from him either. Don't think he has a new chick neither. He'd have brought her to the room and put me out if he did."

"That he would." Rooster had more women in his harem than Blue could name. They were almost an association, helping each other out instead of being jealous. He couldn't fathom it.

"You're the closest thing to a friend he has." The woman peered up at him. "I'm asking you to look for him. He can be a jerk when he's got some new chick, but he's the only one who listens to me."

"Listens?" Blue raised an eyebrow.

"Whatever else he wants, when I talk to him, he listens like I'm the only thing in the world." Tears welled up in her eyes. "It's like I'm more real when I'm with him." She held out a small bundle of cardboard. "These are free McDonald's coffees. It's all I've got."

Blue counted eight in the stack. He took four of them. "I'll do what I can, no promises." The coffee cards went into his jacket pocket. "What's your name?"

"Rooster told the motel my name was Hannah."

"What do you call yourself?"

"Hannah's as good a name as any." She wandered away, and Blue stared after her. Was being a good listener really that big a deal? He put his bet on her wanting to keep her warm room. This year, even in spring, days were still chilly, the night cold. At least today was dry.

***

Blue crossed the street and headed north. He pulled his beanie from a pocket in his coat and put it on. Not much of a disguise, but unless Hank was looking for him, it would get him past Timmies. His stomach grumbled. Maybe the

Sally Ann would still have bread left. The change in his pocket wasn't enough for a muffin.

He almost stopped in at the Big Edition office, but this late in the month the paper didn't sell well. He didn't want to haul around papers nobody'd buy.

Tranquille bustled like two streams that refused to mix. People in well-worn dirty clothes and a crazy mix of layers passed those in clean clothes which, if they had a tear, had been bought that way. Neither met the other's eyes though they miraculously avoided collisions on the sidewalk.

A car honked at a man pushing a shopping cart overflowing with torn black bags and a cardboard sign reading "Bless you." The wave the man responded with didn't look like a blessing.

At the Sally Ann, a stale loaf of rye bread sat on the shelf. Blue picked it up and turned to see a woman eyeing it hungrily and nodded for her to follow him outside where he took a handful of slices before passing the rest to her. On an impulse, he gave her a free coffee coupon from the ones in his pocket.

"You know Rooster?" He stepped back to give her space to dash if she wanted.

"Some." She stuffed bread into her mouth. He nibbled at one of his slices. "Haven't seen him about lately."

"Right. Thanks." Blue smiled and headed toward McDonald's. A coffee was calling his name. He ate the rye bread as he walked, tossing the last crust to a pair of crows.

The girl at the counter relaxed when he handed over the filled cardboard oval for a free coffee. Blue sat in a far corner where management wouldn't spot him, though as long as he had the cup, he was likely safe enough. The caffeine settled into his veins, helping him to both relax and wake up properly.

"Hey." A man with a Santa Claus beard and tattooed arms slid in across from Blue. "You going to keep that sticker? Only need one to fill a card."

Blue peeled it off his cup and passed it over.

"What's up, Sam?"

"Different turkeys, same shit." Sam slurped at his coffee. It almost overflowed from the cream and sugar the man put into it. Blue drank his black and bitter.

"Ain't that the truth." Blue stretched and rolled his neck. A youngster cried, high pitched and sharp, on the other side of the restaurant and Blue gripped his cup to keep his hands from shaking. "You seen Rooster about?"

"Didn't know you swung that way."

"Don't, we're friends, sort of."

"Huh, didn't know he had any." Sam stared into his coffee. "Couple days back he was talking to a woman on the street."

Blue laughed. "When is he not?"

"Didn't look like his usual type."

"He has a type?" Blue ran through the women he knew of who'd been one of Rooster's chicks. They were all ages, shapes, race.

"Didn't look like she needed him." Sam glanced up at Blue. "His women talk on and on about how he listens to them, like they'd die for the chance to pour words into his ear. All of them desperate for his attention."

"Right." Blue leaned back. "So a woman who wasn't desperate."

"Didn't say she wasn't desperate. Had the shakes bad, only not for Rooster if you get me."

The youngster took up its wailing again, accompanied by a woman's cajoling voice.

"Gotta go." Blue stood and picked up his coffee. "Thanks for the help."

Outside he took a long pull at the coffee, wishing again for a drink. The chill breeze curled under his coat collar, making him shiver. Should have asked where Sam had seen Rooster. Too late now.

To keep warm, Blue put his free hand in his pocket and headed toward the North Thompson. He'd check out a couple of places Rooster camped when he wasn't flush enough for a room. Wasn't likely, but what the hell, he didn't have anything else to do.

The wind was sharper by the river, but after Blue clambered down toward the beach, he could walk along the path sheltered by the trees. The water covered the beach but left a dry strip of brush. Though it was early yet, he spotted more than one tent. None of them looked like Rooster's and one fight in a day was enough. He wouldn't risk being thought a trespasser, so he skirted around them. Didn't look like anyone was home anyway.

He rounded the bend and walked under the Overlander Bridge, then up the bank and over to MacDonald Park. Nothing gained but mud on his boots.

The upside was he'd burned enough time to head to The Loop to see what they had on for lunch. He completed his circle back to Tranquille and pushed through the doors. The air carrying the smell of turkey and gravy made his stomach rumble. Blue grabbed a plate and another coffee and tucked in. A few people gossiped over their meals, but most concentrated on eating the only food they'd get that day.

"What's up, Blue?"

"Not a lot, Jake." Blue leaned back to look up at the guy who ran the kitchen and kept things moving. "Looking for Rooster."

"Haven't seen him." Jake frowned. "He's usually in at least once a week."

"One of his chicks is worried." Blue shrugged and wiped his plate with a bit of bread and sighed. "Good as usual."

"Payday tomorrow." Jake said. "You'll find him under a bush hopped up on something."

"Hope so."

Jake moved on to talk to a couple other regulars.

"You hear Ray OD'd?" A woman Blue didn't know was talking to a man on a scooter beside her.

"Ray?" The man shook his head. "Thought he was smarter than that."

"Not smart enough."

Someone pulled out a deck of cards and Blue played cribbage until closing, then helped Jake clean up for the day.

He should head back to his camp. Might as well take another check for Rooster again on the way. Remembering Ray's fate, he peered into places someone might hide to take their hit. Nothing.

Almost at the Halston bridge, Blue reached up to tug on a rope, untying the knot. He lowered his bag to the ground, then tucked both ends of the rope out of sight. Back when he'd thought camping was just a fun activity, he'd learned to hide his gear in trees to keep it away from bears. It worked just as well for people. At least, no one had found it yet.

Across the river, the mountains glowed gold in the late afternoon light. Blue checked the pitiful supply of tinned food he had left. Good thing tomorrow was payday. He sat watching the geese until the sky darkened, and the moon rose to reflect in the river.

The moon was a perfect circle, shining with silver light. He'd like to live up there with no people around. Instead, he was stuck down here with the reflection, troubled by the currents of the world. He shook the thoughts from his head and wrapped up in his bivouac bag, tent and sleeping bag in one.

He fell asleep with the sound of geese honking in the dark.

***

Hank scowled. Tad was a jerk to tell him off in front of his friends, but at least he hadn't ended up a total goof. That weird old guy. If Hank could do that stuff, he wouldn't be holding back.

Trouble was, Hank needed the money Tad paid him for the stupid stuff he had to do. He had no clue why anyone would want to test drugs on random people. You bought the stuff, then sold it, and who cared what happened after that. But arguing with Tad was always a bad idea, even

9

more so when he stomped around in a bad mood. Hank suspected Tad didn't understand any better than Hank did why they were giving away drugs, then monitoring what happened.

The worst was the questions. Who the hell cared how a junkie felt after a fix? But each question had to have an answer circled, and Hank didn't quite dare to randomly assign answers. At least this newest guy liked to talk. The problem was getting him to shut up, but he'd survived a few tests, making him useful. He'd vanished for most of an afternoon, the subject of Tad's tirade.

Now the old man had disappeared again. Hank's palms sweated as he thought about what Tad would do if he found out. Wiping them on the tyvex overalls did nothing to help. They'd been told to wear the suits and the masks all the time around the 'test subjects' Tad called them, with a sneer and a glance over his shoulder as if there was someone behind him he feared.

"The old fart's done a runner." Tad shook Dan. "We've got to go find him before Tad gets back. He'll gut us for sure."

"Gut you," Dan opened one eye. "You're the one he's pissed at."

"If he learns you're sleeping instead of watching…"

"Fine." Dan sat up and adjusted his mask. "Let's get on with it."

The woman subject lay on the mat, only the slight movement of her chest showing she was alive. "She won't be going anywhere." Dan pushed Hank toward the door.

"That's what you said about the old man too."

"How did he get past you?"

"Had to take a leak."

The night air was chilly and misty. The guy couldn't have gone that far.

"You go that way around the park, I'll go this way. Whistle if you spot him."

"Fuck you." Dan said, but walked in the direction Hank pointed.

Luckily, it was well after two in the morning. No one would be around. Hank jogged around the perimeter of the park.

There, something shambling along. In the fog, it could have been a zombie. Hank whistled and ran to head the old man off. Between the two of them, they corralled the escapee and led him back to the building.

Dan pushed him down on the mat.

"Don't move, or I'll slit your throat."

Hank rolled his eyes and kicked the old fucker's ribs.

At least Tad would never find out.

***

Rooster lay in a fog, the drug swirling through his system. Aliens in white walked by and nudging him with their toes, they spoke, but he didn't understand the words.

They left, and he returned to the embrace of the drug.

CHAPTER 2
Friday, April 26

The crows woke him with their racket.

"All right, all right, I'm up already." Blue scrubbed his face with hands dampened by dew on the surrounding leaves.

Even working as slowly as possible, packing up his camp went too quickly. He checked from the River Trail path to be sure his bag didn't stand out. Satisfied, he fingered the change in his pocket; it hadn't multiplied overnight.

Blue refused to panhandle, but he'd be gnawing on his own arms by the end of the weekend. He'd head down toward The Big Edition office, who knows maybe someone hadn't read the paper yet. All he needed was to sell a couple.

He grabbed a quick coffee from the urn, still decent at this time in the morning. Dabra waved at him and went back to whatever she'd been doing on the computer. From the glazed look in her eyes, he suspected laying out the next month's paper.

After taking a bag and shoving a fistful of papers into it, Blue headed out onto Tranquille.

Selling the paper gave him an excuse to stand around, just not too close to doors and out of the way of the people rushing past. Occasionally someone stopped to ask if it was the new edition. One gave him toonie anyway. By the time the sun stood mostly overhead, a few other coins had joined it in his pocket.

"Any sales?" Dabra smiled at him.

"A few," Blue shrugged, and replaced the bag and papers. "Enough for a sandwich."

"There might be something in the fridge. They had a meeting last night, something about expanding the Peer Ambassador Network program." She lifted her eyebrow, but Blue shook his head.

"I'll take the food if it's there, but I'm not good with people. Too much and I get jittery."

"All right then."

Blue found a couple slices of pizza. They looked older than last night's, but he took them anyway. He munched away at them as he walked north.

An ambulance scooted past and into the back alley. Probably an overdose. There were far too many recently. No matter how much people like the Peer Ambassadors worked, there would be people who slipped through the cracks or had plain bad luck.

He followed the ambulance to where the blue-coated paramedics were kneeling over a prone figure. They weren't doing much, so either the person was fine or dead, which was just a different kind of fine.

The paramedics stood and talked a bit more, then shrugged and climbed back into the bus and drove away.

Blue strolled along until he spotted the bundle of clothes huddled in a corner. The man's face was the grey of the concrete behind him, and he mumbled incoherent curses. A needle lay on the ground beside him.

"Wha' you starin' a'" the man lifted his head and fixed Blue with a glare.

"Just passing through." Blue lifted the second slice of pizza. "You want some?" The man stretched out a hand, so Blue ripped a piece off and handed it to him. The man wolfed it down so fast, Blue was afraid he'd puke it up again. But he dropped his head and looked like he'd gone to sleep. Blue finished up his and licked his fingers.

He had enough change to buy something at Timmies. Taking the coffee and muffin into the bathroom. Blue washed as much as he could before someone thought he was shooting up, then scrubbed dry.

Out in the store, Hank sat alone, sulking in the corner.

"I'll take another coffee, double double." Blue carried the cup over and placed in front of Hank.

"What the hell do you want?" Hank sounded more petulant than angry.

"Don't want to be watching for you constantly. Consider this a peace offering."

Hank picked up the cup and sipped at it, made a face and sighed.

"Who'd have thought I'd be taking charity from a bum."

"Peace offering." Blue slurped carefully at his. He pulled the muffin out of the bag and split it to offer a chunk to Hank.

"You got enough to get me out of town?" Hank leaned forward. "There's people mad at me. Not good people."

Blue shook his head.

"Do I look like I have that kind of money?"

Hank sagged into his seat.

Blue finished his coffee and since Hank didn't say anything more, he left the kid to his sulk. If every young punk who thought they were going to be killed, died, Kamloops would be the murder capital of the country.

With nothing better to do, Blue meandered down to MacArthur Island Park, there was a distant chance Rooster had found a new place to crash, though why he'd sleep cold when he still had four days left in a warm room Blue couldn't say. No one ever accused Rooster of being sensible.

All he saw in the bush were deer. They stared back at him boldly. He half expected one to stick its tongue out at him.

Back on Tranquille, Hannah-is-good-enough waited for him. Her hands shook, but her eyes were clear.

"Anything?"

Blue shook his head.

"Sam saw him a couple days back talking to some girl. Said she didn't look like Rooster's type."

Hannah drew her brows together. "Why would he talk to her then? Women are like drugs to him, if he wasn't going to get a fix, he'd ignore her."

"Said she was the one looked like needing a fix."

"Rooster doesn't deal." Hannah slashed her hand down. Blue had to agree with her. He'd never known Rooster to be interested in anything approaching work and dealing did take a little effort.

"I'll keep poking about." Blue said, and Hannah walked away.

Friday on Tranquille was getting crowded, the lucky ones walking into the restaurants looking forward to a meal. Others searched for corners to be alone with their addictions. In between were people travelling from here to there along the shortest route.

It made Blue's guts buzz. He crossed the street and took Oak across to Fortune, then to Schubert. The quiet of the neighbourhood eased the anxiety. A few joggers nodded at him as they passed.

Blue climbed down the bank and took the path. If he tried hard enough, he could convince himself he was in the deep bush with no one in any direction for days.

"Hey Blue," Sam's voice hailed him. Blue stepped through the brush into Sam's camp. A tiny tent with a tarp, a fire set in a large pot. A smaller pot sat on a grate over the fire. He brushed the smoke out of his face and parked himself on a rickety chair across from Sam.

"You find Rooster?" Sam stirred the noodles in the pot. "Tastes like crap without milk and butter, but it's food."

"Get a coffee and muffin and ask for extra milk and butter in the bag. Say it's for someone else."

"Gotta try that."

"When you saw Rooster with that girl, where was he?"

Sam's hands froze, holding the pot to empty the water out, as if he could only either think or move.

"Not far from the Duchess. I think." Sam's hand moved again as he dumped the cheese packet into the pot and stirred it with a fork, then started eating. "Sorry, only got one fork."

"No worries, I had a good day." Blue leaned back and stared up into the trees. Tiny birds flitted about.

"You hear about the ghosts?" Sam's eating stopped as he spoke.

"Ghosts?"

"Some guy said this old place was haunted, swore he saw ghosts running about near MacDonald Park. Idiot. Ghosts aren't real, had to be aliens." He went back to his mac and cheese.

Blue didn't ask any questions. Get Sam on the subject of aliens and UFOs and he'd be here 'til morning. When the other man didn't look up from his pot, Blue stood and slipped away. Sam waved the fork at him in farewell.

CHAPTER 3
Saturday, April 27

Rain woke Blue. Shedding his outer clothes, he crawled out of his bivouac bag, careful to protect the inside from the wet. Since he would get soaked anyway, he dug a sliver of soap from his gear bag and a razor.

The razor was dull enough to make shaving painful, but scruffy cheeks put off some people who would otherwise buy the paper. After shaving, he soaped and rinsed off quickly to avoid an indecency complaint from an early dog walker.

Today he dressed in wool pants and shirt he'd bought at a thrift shop one day he'd been flush. He'd expected to itch terribly, but instead he discovered they were soft and comfortable, and more importantly, warm regardless of whether they were wet or dry. Perfect for this day, though wet wool wasn't his cologne of choice.

A cap from his gear bag protected his head a little. After packing and stashing his gear, he picked up his leather jacket and slipped it on. Keeping it under his sleeping bag kept it safe and made the ground marginally softer.

Hannah waited for him at McDonald's.

"I've found somewhere to go." She pushed more free coffee cards across the table to him. "You don't need to find Rooster now. Let him rot."

When she glanced up at him through her eyelashes, her eyes were red. Then she stood and walked away. A young man opened the door for her. He must have said something because she missed a step and almost fell. The young man laughed and strolled off, hands in his pockets as if it was a beautiful sunny day, not pouring rain.

Blue picked up the stack of coffee cards. Each sticker was exactingly placed. He pulled out the last of the first bunch she'd given him. The stickers were slapped on haphazardly, even overlapping in places. *Strange.*

He finished his drink as slowly as he dared, but a family with noisy kids sent him out into the rain earlier than he wanted. Nothing else to do but wander about, unless he wanted to buy a coffee to sit in the Mall where it was dry.

His feet carried him toward Tranquille. The lights of cars reflected off the wet pavement. Puddles mirrored storefronts and the few people out on the street. It had a different feel to it. Slower, cleaner.

Across the street outside the Timmies, Hank stood under the overhang with his gang of friends. Blue smiled, as he figured, the panic had been over nothing serious. A girl leaned against the wall of the Duchess, huddled in the cold. Impulse made him cross the street to talk to her.

"You look cold." He stood a safe distance away. She looked at him, sizing him up.

"No shit." She wore black jeans, a black t-shirt and a black eye showing through her dusky skin under her black hair. He couldn't tell if the shivering was from the cold or withdrawal. Tracks marked both arms.

"If you aren't going to pay, go to hell, you're cramping my style."

Blue snorted and waved at the all but deserted street.

"You're in the wrong time zone, kid."

"You want some?" She pulled her t-shirt tighter, only emphasizing how young she looked. Maybe that was the plan.

"Not in the market."

"Got a friend who can do you if you swing that way."

"Don't swing at all, kid." Blue took the stack of free coffees Hannah had given him and pushed it into her hand. The regimented stickers made him nervous.

"What the f..." She stared at the cards, but shoved them into her back pocket. "You're the dude looking for Rooster."

"I was." Blue held back from stepping out into the rain.

"Someone said he had a line on new blow. Wicked stuff. Said he didn't, but he was lying."

"That was a few days back?"

"Yeah, the asshole blew me off." She waved at the street. "I had to get a fix on the installment plan."

"Right." Blue pushed away from the wall.

"Find him for me," the girl said, "I want to kick his ass."

"If I see him, I'll let him know."

Blue wandered the streets off of Tranquille, heading toward MacDonald Park. There'd be shelter there and no one would run him off. He passed a house looking run down, boards over windows and unkempt yard.

Neighbours must love that place.

Where the rain had transformed Tranquille into something different, it only made the park feel lonelier. He huddled against the wall of the pumphouse for the water park. Even his wool clothes couldn't keep the chill from his bones. He might have to try the Emerald, but just thinking it gave him the shakes.

"I'd say you was jonesing for a hit if I didn't know you was the most boring man on the planet." Rooster slumped against the wall beside Blue.

"Been looking for you."

"So I heard." Rooster shrugged and stared into the rain. "Stupid."

"Nothing better to do."

"Still stupid." Rooster put his head on his knees. "I'm dead, Blue. A ghost, plan to stay that way."

"What killed you?"

"The aliens have the best shit. Call it Black Death. Crazy, never had anything like it."

"That's something coming from you."

"No shit."

"That reminds me, a kid at the Duchess wants to kick your ass."

"All in black?"

"Including her eye."

Rooster glared at Blue. "You know I never hit women."

"Didn't say you did." Blue sighed. "Hannah told me she's got no need of you."

"Good." Rooster pushed himself to his feet and tottered slightly. "Drink a beer in my memory." He staggered off into the rain.

Blue compromised that evening. He set up under the Halston bridge, huddled in a corner where he'd be hard to see.

CHAPTER 4

"Hey, you can't be sleeping there." The bylaws officer looked more bored than angry.

"I'm awake now." Blue stretched and crawled out of the bag. Close enough to morning now, anyway.

"Fine then." The officer walked away.

Blue rolled up his gear. The wool clothes had pretty much dried overnight, so he kept his usual jeans and shirt on under the leather. He'd have to find a better place to stash his gear. The bylaws people could be sharp eyed, and not all were as understanding.

At least the rain had stopped. He shouldered his bag and headed south. There were other places the trees were thick enough to hide his bag.

A crowd under the Overlander pawed at something. They took off when one of them saw Blue and shouted. Blue climbed up to investigate. Rooster lay twisted, cold and blue. A rubber band circled his arm, and a needle lay beside him.

Blue shuffled back, losing his balance and rolling down the slope.

"You okay?" A young woman with a dog and a stroller stared at him wide eyed. The dog yapped, then came over to lick his face.

"You have a phone?" Blue let the dog continue to wash his face until the woman pulled it back.

"Yes." She lifted it out of the stroller.

"Call the police." Blue shuddered and lay strengthless on the dirt. "There's a body up there." He waved vaguely.

"Don't look, just call. Trust me, that's something you don't need to see."

The toddler in the stroller pushed a half-eaten package of crackers at him. "Snack?"

He fought to a sitting position and took the bag. Nibbling on them helped fight back the nausea. The woman absentmindedly handed him a juice box and one to the boy in the stroller, then opened another package of crackers.

Blue and the child shared them as the sirens got closer, then died with a final gargle. The boy laughed and pointed at the officers as they walked under the bridge holding flashlights. The woman waved them over.

The world spun around Blue, and he dropped his head to his knees.

CHAPTER 5
Sunday, April 28

"He said the body's up there." The woman's voice spoke from a distance. Blue tried to remember what had happened. Other voices shouted for backup, for a bus. Then they were asking him questions, yelling at him, asking him...

"Let's get you out of here." A different woman said, and a hand hoisted him to his feet. "Breathe, don't think about anything but breathing." She wore a blue uniform, but if he didn't look at her, it might be all right. His heart slowed. He wasn't there. That was over and done a long time ago.

"That's better." Something warm filled his hand. "Drink up, sorry if you don't like it sweet." Coffee ran down his throat like liquid sugar.

"There has to be more sugar than coffee in this." Blue finished the cup and she refilled it.

"A lot of people drink it like that for the boost."

Hank making a face at the double double came to Blue's mind. "I guess so." She guided him over to sit in the open door of a cruiser. He pretended it was just some car and believed it enough not to panic again.

"Had to be a shock finding a body." She refilled his cup from a thermos.

"Not the first time." Blue stared into the cup.

"Must be hard." The cop poured herself a cup and leaned against the car. She had positioned them so her body was between him and her gun. Smart. Somehow, she made the blue uniform look, if not friendly, at least less intimidating. Red hair pulled into a ponytail framed blue eyes filled with compassion.

"Isn't supposed to be easy." Blue emptied the cup in one drink and handed it to her. "He was a friend."

"Makes it that much worse."

She was the strangest cop he'd met. No questions, no stare sizing him up, just crappy coffee and sympathy.

"I'm Constable Madoc with Car 40." She put his cup on the roof of the cruiser. "My partner's a psych nurse, he's talking to the woman and her boy. The other guys will get to taking your statement in a bit. In the meantime, I want you to relax and concentrate on breathing."

"My bag will be somewhere under the bridge." Blue's hand clenched on his leg. "That's everything I own."

Constable Madoc mumbled into her radio and after a moment she turned to Blue.

"They found a bag halfway down the slope. No need to keep it as evidence. Just identify what's in it."

"Sleeping bag, wool pants, shirt, other shit."

She mumbled more, then pointed to where a man in jeans and a dress shirt carried it toward them.

"John's got it for you. One less bit of paperwork."

John dropped it at Blue's feet and gave him a scan from boots to cap, then sat himself in another cruiser and set to making notes.

Another officer escorted the woman and her stroller and dog out into the light, handed her a card, then returned under the bridge.

Blue watched as officers came and went, a couple men loaded the body into a van, but didn't drive away yet. Finally, one of the officers came over.

"You okay to give your statement, sir?"

Blue laughed. "Haven't been 'sir' for a long time. Call me Blue."

"Very well then, Blue, tell me what happened in your own words."

Blue took the officer through the moment up to finding Rooster, then his tumble down the hill and the woman calling 911.

"Very cogent," the officer said. "You've done this before."

Blue froze and fought back nausea.

"Sorry, that was cavalier." The officer frowned. "If there is nothing else?"

"Rooster was a friend, or a close to one as he would allow." Blue concentrated on the ground between the officer's dusty black boots. "He was up for any kind of high. He'd swallow pills, eat mushrooms, smoke crack, whatever, but he was deathly afraid of needles. Just seeing one on the ground made him queasy."

"You suggesting he wasn't the one to stick the needle in his arm?"

"I'm suggesting he wouldn't let anyone stick him with a needle while he was alive, not if he saw it coming."

The officer grunted. "Thank you for the information. You called him Rooster, do you know his real name?"

"Sorry, haven't a clue."

The officer grunted again.

"Any way we can get hold of you if we need to talk to you?"

"Leave a message with Jake at The Loop or Dabra at The Big Edition, I see them most weekdays."

"No need to keep you around any longer. Can I give you a ride somewhere?"

"Thanks, but I'm good."

The officer snapped his notebook closed, then dug out his wallet. He handed Blue two cards.

"One's my business card if you think of something else for us. The other's a meal at my sister's sandwich shop."

"Thank you." Blue peered at the card. He knew the place. It was a good spot to walk past just before closing.

"She likes to do what she can."

"I mean for treating me like a person, not a bum."

"No problem. Appreciate your help." The cop nodded and walked over to chat with John in the other car.

"I'd better hoof it." Blue pushed himself up, testing his balance for a second before taking a step.

"Here's my card as well." Constable Madoc handed it to him. "Take care of yourself."

"Thanks, see you around." Blue shouldered his bag and headed north, he'd have to circle around to get where he planned to go, and as nice as the cops had been, he didn't want them watching him go.

If he had his way, he'd never talk to them again. He felt the cards in his pocket and was tempted to chuck them into the first trash can he passed, but she'd given him coffee and he'd passed on that free meal. The least he could do was carry their cards for a bit.

***

Blue stared at the lights on the river, he'd found a place to crash covered by some heavy brush.

A tall can of beer chilled his hand. He imagined the bitter coolness, felt the slight buzz. Just one beer, Rooster had asked him. The can crackled in his grip. Damn, but he wanted this drink.

"Sorry, Rooster." Blue popped open the beer, then poured it into the river before crushing the can. "Can't do it. Going to need my head on straight. Aliens, huh?"

Some kids with a loud party kept him awake until police came and shooed them away. Then an amorous couple kept it up for a ridiculously long time.

Even when it was quiet, his eyes wouldn't close. Rooster's blue face accused him.

"Damn it, Rooster, you're nothing but trouble."

Tomorrow he'd try to pick up more gossip about those aliens. Wasn't like he had anything better to do.

***

Hank hunched over the newest subject, trying not to hear the argument from the other side of the partial wall.

"Was dumping him such a good idea?" Tad's nervous voice made him shiver. Hank didn't want to deal with the person who scared that psycho. "Hannah had his friend looking for him."

"He was a known drug user, they might do a cursory tox screen, but nothing to cause us any problems." The woman's voice grew sharper. "You said you'd dealt with that situation."

28

"She told him she was fine, and he didn't need to look. Handed him those free coffees you gave me."

"And her?"

"Working for me, she's older, but some don't care about that."

"How is the new subject working out?"

"She hasn't died, yet." The man frowned. "I don't get all this fuss anyway."

"Dead people don't buy drugs. We need to get a safe dosage to sell, then we get the repeat business. Much easier to sell to someone who knows us than find new customers."

"You sound like some kind of salesman."

"My father's money bought me a business degree, among other things."

Hank pushed himself up. He wanted to wipe the sweat off his face, but Tad had already yelled at him once for taking the mask off. The table with the white powder pulled his attention. That's what these 'subjects' were taking.

The old man had died, and he wasn't the first. Though he'd caused more trouble than anyone else by constantly running off, Hank didn't like that he died. This letting people die of overdoses bothered him more than the idea of stabbing or beating someone. Maybe Tad was right, and he was a wuss.

Dan lounged on the chair, mask pushed up on his forehead again. He'd done a line from the table, daring Hank to say anything. Asshole.

Hank stomped over and kicked the chair. Dan fell bonelessly to the floor.

"Shit!"

"Keep it quiet." Tad came around the wall. His fists clenched, eyes glittering above his own mask.

Hank pointed to Dan on the floor.

"I think he's dead."

The woman wore a full face mask, and it muffled her voice.

"The idiot did a line from the pure stuff. Deal with it." She turned away and went back around the wall. A car started up as the garage door creaked open. It shut again with a thump.

"You know what to do." Tad came back into the room.

Hank took Dan's phone. The idiot didn't need it. Too bad there was no wifi in this place. Dan didn't have data, but he could get internet at Timmies.

Hank wrapped Dan in the tarp, Nolan, Tad's second, would come by with his old truck and they'd go looking for a corner to leave the body. Each time, Hank sweated that a cop would stop them and find the body, but Nolan said the cops were doing paperwork after 3am, and they'd never seen a cruiser.

It didn't stop Hank from worrying.

CHAPTER 6
Monday, April 29

The rain started as Blue walked south and west toward Tranquille. He stopped under the shelter of a tree and debated the wisdom of returning to his camp and hiding out from the wet. By the time he got back there he'd be cold and damp anyway, not to mention he'd have to deal with sitting with his thoughts while he waited out the weather.

He kept going. The gear would be dry, he could change when he got back and find somewhere more sheltered for the night. The rain looked to hang around a while. Not good weather for selling papers. Maybe he'd go to The Loop and hang out.

People scurried past with umbrellas or raincoats, huddled against the chill. No one paid much attention to anything but avoiding being splashed by passing cars.

If he hadn't bought that beer for Rooster, he'd have enough for a coffee and muffin at Timmies, but he could get something at The Loop and give Jake a hand.

Someone sat against a wall, water pooling around them. That didn't look good. Blue walked over and checked. The man's face was deathly pale, and he wasn't sure the guy had a pulse. His wrist was cold and clammy. Blue ran into a store.

"There's a guy out front looks like he over-dosed."

"I'll call 911." The woman behind the counter picked up a phone and handed Blue a black case. "The boss makes us keep a Nalaxone kit handy. You know how to use it?"

"I do." Blue took the kit and ran back outside. He filled the needle and punched it into the man's leg administering a dose. There was a pulse, but very weak when he checked the man's neck.

Blue moved the man, so his head didn't fall forward and make it hard to breathe. The backpack made a handy thing to hold up his shoulders. His pulse had disappeared.

A crowd gathered around.

"Anyone know CPR?" Blue called without turning around.

"I'll do compressions." A young woman came forward and moved the man's heavy coat out of the way.

Blue filled the man's lungs with air three times, then the woman worked on compressions. She was moving like she'd done it many times before, many people dithered about before using enough force.

Sirens approached, and an ambulance pulled up. Blue didn't know how long they'd worked, but the woman had to be tired and he felt lightheaded. Paramedics took over from him. So Blue crawled over to the wall and sat against it until the world gave up tilting a few degrees off plumb.

The flashing lights of the ambulance reflected on the wet sidewalk, making the scene alternate between grey and red. The paramedics worked on the man, then one fetched the stretcher. They lifted the man on it and loaded him in the back of the vehicle. The siren wailed as the ambulance drove away. Blue stood, but his head felt fine now. He picked up the backpack and carried it into the store.

"They didn't take this, maybe put it behind the counter in case the guy comes back for it."

"Why would he?" The woman looked doubtfully at the grubby and torn pack with the toe of a running shoe sticking from a hole.

"It might be all he has in the world." Blue held it up. "Likely it's junk, but it's his junk."

"All right then, I'll keep it for a week." She took it reluctantly, touching only with the tips of her fingers, but placed it carefully in a corner out of the way. "I'll make a note."

"Appreciate it."

"You know him?" The woman asked.

"No, but not that long ago it could have been me." Blue looked out the window at the rain. "Better get going."

The woman's eyes followed him through the window as he headed south.

Could have been me? Blue shook his head. Rooster was getting to him. He'd left the desire to leave this world behind with the booze. At least he thought he had, but as he walked, rain working its way down his back, he had to admit he envied Rooster and that nameless man whatever peace they found in their exit from this world.

The drink had given him a goal each day. Make or steal enough to get drunk. When he'd given up the booze, the days grew longer and slower without that something to work toward. In two years of not drinking, he'd yet to find a good substitute. Merely making it from morning to night didn't hold his attention with the same intensity.

***

He'd been drinking with a buddy. In those days anyone with alcohol was a buddy. The guy had been a loud and obnoxious drunk, taking more of the mickey than Blue, but he'd lifted the bottle so Blue guessed he had the right.

The whole argument was senseless, but the guy with the bottle started something with a few young punks. The kind who wore denim and leather, but bought it new with cash and drove their father's cars if they didn't have their own. The obnoxious drunk took a swing at one for some reason, next thing all three were pushing the guy around. Blue didn't care since he was holding the bottle.

One of them shoved the guy, or he'd tripped and fallen on his own. It didn't matter in the end. His head met a rock with a hollow sound. The punks beat a quick retreat. Blue had almost finished the bottle, but felt bad for not sharing, so he went to give his buddy the last gulp.

Blood had splashed on the rock and the ground around it. The guy's eyes stared blindly upward with a puzzled expression on his face, like he couldn't figure out what happened. Blue poured the last of the booze into the guy's mouth, but he didn't swallow. The fact of the man's death slowly percolated into Blue's mind. For reasons he still didn't understand, the realization terrified him. He'd shaken and fallen to his knees, then crawled away to hide in the brush where he'd shivered through the night.

In the early morning he'd woken to start the search for the next day's intoxication, carefully avoiding looking toward where the body lay. All day he'd panhandled, and by some stroke of fortune did well enough to buy a bottle and drown his existence for another day. He bought a cheap bottle and hid where he wouldn't have to share. At the first taste of alcohol, the man's face came into his mind. The image wouldn't go away, no matter how many slugs from the bottle Blue took.

The terror came back worse than before. He could die just as easily by tripping over a stone. Despite having no real reason to live, and plenty of reasons to die, he'd never been able to take that last step. Now it sent him shaking and weeping to even consider his death.

Blue hitchhiked away from that town, ending up in Kamloops with little more than a small bag and a spare t-shirt. In Kamloops he didn't drink and gradually built up his gear to where he could be relatively comfortable in most weather. Now he made most of his extra income from selling The Big Edition, not panhandling.

The hardest thing was the part of him that still wanted a drink, that didn't care about anything but blotting out the hardness of life. He'd learned to set it aside, but it was a constant battle.

***

Blue arrived at The Loop and walked in. Jake waved him over and Blue poured himself a coffee, putting his jacket to dry in the back room where it wouldn't walk away.

"You look about a seven on the drowned rat scale." Jake handed him a bowl of soup.

"OD on the way here." Blue sat down to eat the soup, crumbling a handful of crackers into it.

"He make it?"

"They went away with sirens going." Blue shrugged and stared up at the ceiling. "But I'm guessing he won't."

"Finish your soup and I'll put you to work for a bit. Get your mind off things." Jake went back into the kitchen.

Blue scraped his bowl clean and carried it and his coffee cup to the back. He settled into the rhythm of chopping as Jake prepared food for the afternoon meal.

People came and went. New people filled out membership forms, pleased to hear there was no cost.

"You should come and help more." Jake bustled about, keeping his eye on half a dozen things at once.

"I should." Blue stretched and scraped another pile of potato pieces into a pot.

Somebody was helping people with computer questions. Blue hadn't touched a computer since... He redirected his thoughts. No good reason to go there.

The day passed, not quickly, but Blue wasn't bored. The work just didn't call to him like it did for Jake. The man probably spent as much time at The Loop as he did at home. His wife Marie ran the front. She was unassuming, but no one argued with her.

Blue headed out before it got too late in the afternoon. The rain wasn't going to stop anytime soon, and it would be easier to move his stuff in the light. He crossed the street to avoid passing by the store where the guy had been that morning. A few people held soggy cardboard signs. Even with The Big Edition, some chose to sit and beg. Blue would never go back.

He picked up his gear and moved under the Halston bridge. If he kept to the top shadowed part again, he might get lucky and avoid being moved along. As it grew darker, it became easier to hide.

The drumming of the rain, along with the howl of tires and the clanking of trains, kept him company through the night.

In the morning, Blue felt as grey as the weather. Seeing that OD the day before had brought back things he usually avoided. He envied Jake, who knew what he wanted to do with his day. Blue floated through life. Looking for Rooster had been a cure for boredom, not a real desire to find the man. If he followed through on seeking the 'aliens' it would be for the same reason.

Now that he'd kicked booze, boredom was the great enemy. Heading down to The Loop would give him something to do. Only he didn't feel like being with people. Other people could call in sick on bad days, then pull the covers over their heads and go back to sleep.

Not Blue, nor any other person living without a secure home. No one would bring him a coffee or keep him company in his doldrums. He crawled out of his bag and rolled it up securely. He couldn't stay under the bridge all day. Even if no one reported him, it would drive him deeper into the despair which clawed at him.

He didn't bother putting his gear up out of the way. Slinging the bag over his shoulder, he headed out into the rain. Walking south on the River Trail, he passed a few dedicated dog walkers, but kept his head down. There was nowhere he wanted to go, so any path would get him there.

River Trail took him over the Thompson and along to Riverside Park, then under the rail bridge and the Red Bridge. He couldn't remember the last time he'd been on the south shore. Surely at least once since he'd arrived in town, he'd crossed the river, but it wouldn't come to his mind. Everything and everyone he knew centered on the North Shore. Even the weather was different with dry pavement and no rain.

Since he was here, he might as well look around. He walked back along Victoria admiring the mix of shops. More people moved around on the street. It had a different feel than Tranquille. Someone came out of a coffee shop and handed him a cup of coffee and a muffin.

"You looked like you needed a little pick me up." The girl smiled at him. Her boyfriend on her arm didn't look surprised or concerned.

"Thank you." Blue smiled for the first time in the day. "You wouldn't believe how much this means to me today."

"You might be surprised." The girl looked up at her boyfriend and the obvious love in their eyes almost brought tears to his. They waved and wandered east, already talking about the next thing.

Blue didn't mind that they'd forgotten him already. She'd noticed him and even for a few seconds cared enough to give him a tiny bit of hope. The gloom in his heart cracked slightly. The hot coffee, very different than Timmies or McDonald's opened it wider.

The muffin had been warmed up. The chocolate chunks had softened to run over his tongue. He didn't often get chocolate. A young man walked along the street with a bag, picking up cigarette butts and other trash with a broom and dustpan, undeterred by damp air.

Blue stopped to chat with the man for a few moments and learned he'd been cleaning the street for quite a while, his personal contribution to the city. More than a few people waved or nodded as they passed.

On the walk back across the bridge, Blue wondered what he was doing. Day by day survival took a lot of effort, but others went beyond that to create a place for themselves. What could he do to give his life a purpose?

The idea of a purpose made him strangely uncomfortable. Blue wasn't sure why, but like a scab half pulled off the question kept coming back to annoy him. He arrived back at the Halston Bridge still with no answer. He finally shoved the question out of his mind.

A few young people were sharing a bong, Blue didn't care for the smell, but they left him alone, so he ignored them. The rain stopped as the sun set, and Blue found a place to crash. He curled up in his bag and closed his eyes until his mind finally stopped asking him unanswerable questions and let him sleep.

CHAPTER 7
Wednesday, May 1

After the two days of drenching rain, the sun came out and Blue arrived early at The Big Edition office to pick up a bag and a bundle of papers. Others stood around drinking coffee, but he just waved at them and headed out to catch the morning rush and take advantage of the weather.

Selling papers gave him a chance to talk to people. He didn't want to forget how to carry on a conversation. Seen too many who couldn't communicate off the street.

More importantly this morning, it gave him an excuse to dawdle along the sidewalk, listening in on groups of youth, or adults clustered around overfilled shopping carts.

The youth were filled with the usual bluster and drama. This one angered that one. How they would beat the enemy with fists, clubs, knives. Sometimes they'd follow through. Most often they were toughest only in their own mind.

"You hear they found Dan dead with a needle in his arm?" The speaker was behind Blue.

"Yes, sir, the paper is three dollars, it helps me feed myself for the month." Blue held up this month's paper, the front cover a picture of a bear eating out of someone's backyard compost pile. The man gave him a five and waved off the change. The young people behind him had moved onto a different subject.

He kept moving north on Tranquille, but overheard no more tidbits. When his bundle got low and his pockets bulged with change and small bills, Blue took the bus back south to the credit union to deposit the money. The Big Edition had worked some magic to get accounts for vendors and others who earned money without a safe place to keep it.

"MacDonald Park is haunted." An old man across the aisle was clearly carrying on an argument from the frustration on his face and the disbelief on his woman companion's.

"Nonsense, just some kids pulling a prank. Like that clown nonsense last year. They probably saw some video on YouTube."

"Al saw it himself when he was walking Fluffy."

"George, Al is half-blind in one eye and can't see out of the other. How'd he be able to tell if it was ghosts or kids?"

"Fluffy would protect Al from kids."

"We talking about the same Fluffy who laid on his bed and watched someone burgle Al's house?"

The argument slid over to the break-in and whether the neighbourhood was getting worse. A couple of people bought papers from Blue went he got off the bus.

Putting money in the bank necessitated digging out his overly thin wallet. He put twenty in to keep him for a while, then banked the rest. The three business cards reminded him he had a free sandwich coming to him. After dropping off the bag and few remaining papers at the office, he walked south to the sandwich shop. The girl behind the counter smiled when she handed her the card and took his order for a beef sandwich.

When she came out to bring him the plate and the iced tea he'd asked for, she put a cookie on a napkin beside the plate and gave him another smile.

He could have lived for days on that one sandwich. It wouldn't keep, so he finished it, but slid the cookie into his pocket.

"You shouldn't give out free meals, it only encourages them." A woman in a power suit frowned at Blue as she placed her order.

"He's not a 'them'." The girl's smile stayed on her face, but her eyes were frosty. "He's a customer." The woman looked away. Halfway through watching her meal being prepared, she turned and walked out. Unperturbed, the girl put the sandwich in a bag and gave it to Blue.

"We can't sell it to someone else once it's made. She deliberately waited, thinking it would bug me. Keep it for later or give it to a friend."

"Thanks." The thought of eating that woman's sandwich made him queasy, he'd pass it on.

Though he'd finished his meal, she made no attempt to hurry him along. He learned her name was Sandra from the regulars who came through. An older woman came in and headed straight to Blue. He stood up, but she waved at him to sit down again.

"How was your meal?" She sat across from him. "I'm Claudia, the owner."

"This is what it would be like to be rich." Blue scanned the shop. "Eating in one meal what would keep me for days, not thinking about how to pay for it. Not having to rush away."

"Hmmm." Claudia tilted her head thoughtfully. "What would could you and your friends afford to pay for a smaller meal?"

"Depends on the day." Blue played with his empty iced tea can. "Some days I'll have five or six bucks in my pocket, others, not a dime. But I think a three dollar meal would be nice. Enough to get me through the day."

"I've been thinking about a low-cost menu. I appreciate your input."

"Everybody knows you're good people." Blue pushed back from the table. "It's nice." He stood up. "I don't want to take up your table all day."

Claudia shrugged, but went back to chat with Sandra. Blue picked up the extra sandwich and headed back out. He handed it to two women sharing a cigarette, one with a baby stroller full of clothes. They stared at him, then took it and went back to their conversation about the evil people who took their kids away.

Blue stopped into Surplus Herby's to buy a new pair of socks, his had worn through. Wallet thinner and the socks stuffed into his jacket pocket, he headed over to MacDonald Park. Maybe sitting around in the park would get him more tidbits of information about aliens.

Hannah stood looking like she was waiting for someone, but when Blue walked in her direction, she left, glancing back at him as she went.

He sat on a bench and watched people walking dogs. Some looked like they were getting the community garden into shape for the season. No one looked worried about ghosts or aliens. What would ghosts want here, anyway? As the woman said, probably kids playing a prank. Blue took out the cookie and nibbled on it.

When the woman stopped in front of him, he took a moment to place her.

"You look better today." She held the dog on a leash, but no toddler in a stroller today.

"Thanks." Blue sighed and tried to decide if he should stand to talk on the same level as her. Laziness won. "Bodies can be like ghosts, they'll haunt you for a while."

She gave him a quizzical look. "You've found more than one?"

Blue's pulse jumped into panic mode, and he tried to hide the sudden tremble in his hand.

"Sorry, I shouldn't pry." She slackened the leash to let the dog sniff at Blue's feet. He scratched its ears. "Curtis is having nightmares. He's afraid of the dark because the scary thing was up in the shadow."

"The cops gave you a card for victim services?" Blue asked.

"Yes, but..."

"Call them, they'll help."

"How do you know?"

"They gave me a card too." Blue thought of Constable Madoc.

"All right then." She tugged on the leash. "Take care." The dog had to scamper to keep up with her. He'd scared her.

After time to let the shakes subside, Blue stood and headed back toward Tranquille.

The vision hit without warning. A room, all in red, the iron smell of blood mixed with other things. The taste of the bile he swallowed back.

You killed us; you killed us. The litany ran through his head in the shrill scream of terrified children. He shouldn't have been talking about bodies. He should have drunk the beer and gone on whatever bender he could afford. Blue's chest hurt and he couldn't get enough air.

He didn't know he'd fallen until the ground slammed into him, but arms and legs refused to work.

"Is he having a heart attack?"

"No, an overdose."

"Clear a space." A sharp pain in his leg tore a howl from him, but at least it shattered the vision. He fought his way to hands and knees, then to his feet. Blurred faces stared at him. Couldn't see the condemnation in their eyes, but he didn't need to.

Blue lurched into motion any direction as long as it was *away*.

He found a corner between a wall and stairs, a dumpster added another screen to hide behind. Air rasped at his throat, and his heart banged painfully. Nausea slowly subsided as exhaustion weighted his eyelids.

***

Someone pawed at his pockets. Blue grabbed the hand and applied a wrist lock.

"Shit." The person scrambled back.

"Told you to leave him alone."

"Should we do him too?"

"He's just some drunk, no one will believe him, but two would be suspicious."

Footsteps receded at a run. Blue fought against the fog. *Where am I?* He pushed himself up and recognized the back alley. Everything he wore was damp and clinging to him, stinking of fear and garbage. Leaning against the wall, he stumbled south. Too dangerous to stay here.

As he walked, he grew steadier, but the sun lightened the sky in the east when he reached his camp. Blue lowered his bag, then changed his clothes. The ones he wore reeked, so he bundled them up to wash or get rid of later, for the moment he stashed them out of smelling range.

After making sure his bag was safe, and holding his wallet, Blue sat against a big tree and put his head on his knees.

Those ghosts would never stop making him pay.

***

This stupid place and its stupid people. Hank wanted the money Tad was supposed to pay him for babysitting the junkies, but he kept coming up with excuses. He figured he was due a couple hundred. That would get him to Vancouver or Calgary, somewhere he'd get the respect he deserved.

The woman didn't look good, and something stunk. No one told him that happened when people died, it never did in the movies. At least she was lying on a tarp already. He checked her pulse, but the clammy skin of her wrist told him he wouldn't find it.

"Got another one, just fricking perfect." Hank kicked the body, though Tad would have had his ass if he'd seen.

Tad wasn't there. Hank kicked it again just to spite the asshole, then wrapped her in the tarp.

Nolan showed up as he always did at the dead part of the morning. They loaded the corpse, then Hank raised the garage door to let the truck out, lowering it and locking it before going out through the door, double checking it was locked too. Tad threatened to gut anyone who left it open.

They pulled up some place behind a building on Tranquille, rolled her out of the tarp, then put it in the toolbox in the truck. Hank tripped over a pair of legs. Some guy blasted out of his mind. Maybe he had a few bills Hank could swipe.

Hank had almost pissed himself when the drunk grabbed him. Nolan laughed, he'd be telling that story at every excuse now. Shit. Couldn't a guy get a break? Hard to show his stuff with people laughing about how stupid he'd looked. All he needed was a decent stake and he would blow this place so fast.

Nolan dropped him back where they were doing their market research. Funny thing to call the process of killing people, then dialing back the dose to not quite kill the next test junkie. Hank pulled the now not-so-white tyvex on and settled his mask in place before walking through to the other room.

Pay or not, Tad expected Hank to do the work. The boss woman reached a whole new level of cold, and she terrified Hank. Hell, even Tad was nervous around her. He picked up the clipboard and wrote the time down, wishing they bought him a phone instead of the cheap watch.

Should have done it when he found her dead. Better late than never.

He stretched out in a corner. Nobody would be awake to let him crash at their place, but sleep was sleep.

CHAPTER 8
Thursday, May 2

Shivering woke Blue up. He had fallen asleep sitting against the tree, still clutching his bag and wallet. Blue crawled into the sleeping bag and tried to fall asleep again.

His mind wouldn't let him rest. Like a hamster on a wheel, it replayed all the mistakes he'd ever made. When he forced his thoughts away from that, it created new scenarios of disaster. People died around in the worst of ways, and he was powerless to prevent it.

Sunrise sent beams of light into his eyes, and he groaned. He hadn't woken feeling this bad since his drinking days. Geese honked on the river, floating downstream a while before flying back up to where they'd started.

The currents of his mind carried him, and he couldn't escape them. He shivered and pulled the sleeping bag closer around him. It felt like he had a fever. Groping in his bag produced a half bottle of water he drank too quickly.

The sun rose higher and he couldn't find the strength to move. He didn't know what he'd do if bylaws showed up, but the day passed at a snail's pace. Fog filled his mind with vague shapes of monsters and horrors. Children screaming turned out to be youngsters walking past with their parents.

The shot of adrenaline and pounding heart had him out of the sleeping bag, so he packed up and stashed his gear. If he did nothing, he'd be awake all night. He should go to The Loop and get something to eat, but the thought of interacting with people made his headache worse. Instead, he walked north along the river, then up the mountain. Anything to bring exhaustion.

The landscape was beautiful, the view breathtaking, but he didn't pay attention. Blue plodded along until the sun began lowering in the west. He headed back, but night caught him before he'd got off the plateau. Huddled in a hollow, Blue waited out the night, dozing in between intervals of jumping and slapping his sides to keep warm.

In the morning he kept walking back to his camp, dug out a tin of chili and ate it cold. Crows squabbled in the trees. Tiny birds flitted about. Blue sat, his mind as empty as it had been full the day before. Thoughts required too much effort, so he stopped trying.

Another day had passed. Blue crawled into his sleeping bag. As soon as he closed his eyes, sleep took him.

CHAPTER 9
Saturday, May 4

"Another OD." Sam stirred his coffee and shook his head. "Found a woman in the alley behind the pawnshop. Still had a needle in her arm."

Blue frowned, he should remember something about that alley.

"They're supposed to be doing something about this opioid thing." Sam frowned and looked around as if the 'they' might be listening.

"Education only reaches those willing to be educated." Blue rubbed his leg. He'd bumped into Sam at Timmies, the first social interaction he'd had in two days.

"Ain't that the truth." Sam slurped his coffee, leaving droplets on his beard. "Heard there's a thing. Heard some kids talking about a new fix, Black Death or something. Can't imagine putting something like that in my system. Give me a bottle of rye, and I'm good." He laughed and drank more coffee.

"Never seen you drunk." Blue's black coffee was still too hot to drink.

"Twenty years sober." Sam pulled out a keychain to show Blue the medallion. "But if it was going to be anything, it would be rye."

"Two years, I think." Blue tapped his finger on the table, then put his hand on his leg to hide it. The topic of booze made him nervous.

"Good on you." Sam grinned at him. "Twenty years or two, it's still one day at a time."

"Some days are harder than others."

"Heard Rooster died under the bridge."

"Yeah." Blue clenched his fist to stop his hand twitching.

"Breathe." Sam's blue eyes held understanding. "Slow it down, bring air all the way into your gut."

Blue tried, and to his surprise the tension eased.

"Lot of people hit the drugs 'cause they're stressed, if you find other ways of dealing with it." Sam shrugged and wiped coffee off his beard. "You need to talk, I got time."

"I'll keep that in mind." Blue wanted no part of talking about what was stressing him. "You hear any more about those aliens of yours?"

Sam nodded, then played with his coffee.

"Not really. People are telling all kinds of strange stories, some are claiming it's ghosts, but they aren't like the aliens who took me."

"How so?"

Sam leaned over the table and whispered as if people might be listening. "The ones that snatched me hooked me up to a machine and asked questions. Gave a nasty shock if they didn't like the answer. Lies, jokes, sarcasm all were forbidden. This crew, what are they about? Nobody's been taken, no strange sickness, nothing. Why come all this way only to hang out and scare a few morons?"

"Seems reasonable, even aliens need motivation."

Sam glared at him, then relaxed when Blue didn't laugh or crack a smile. "Chances are we won't like it when we do find out." He stood up. "Coffee's empty, gotta take a leak then hit the street."

Blue sipped at his own drink, now at a comfortable temperature.

Motivation. What was his? He'd looked for Rooster mostly to alleviate boredom, not out of any concern for Rooster. His short-lived determination to search out the aliens was a distraction from the memories threatening his sanity. Curing boredom could drive him insane, or worse, to drink again.

Whatever was going on, Blue would leave it alone. Boredom wouldn't kill him.

He walked south to The Big Edition office to pick up a bag and papers. Both time of day and month were wrong for good selling, but it would be worth the effort. The place was closed. Saturday, Blue swore. He had a little change in his pocket, but his bank card was with his gear hidden away, he'd have to walk up to his camp, back near Halston, and pick up the card.

Shouting drew his attention as he walked. Another fight at Timmies. Some skinny kid getting a beating from someone in new jeans and a shiny leather jacket. Not a kid, the girl from outside the Duchess. Blue crossed the street. The crowd parted when he snarled at them to move.

"Butt out, old man." The punk pointed at Blue. Of course, he'd seen Hank's humiliation.

"Don't feel like it." Blue kept his hand loose at his hips and strolled causally toward him. "Don't like bullies."

"She owes me money." More whine than bluster now.

"Tough." Blue held the punk's gaze, checking the reflection in the windows to watch his back. The punk swore and pushed through the crowd. Something about him felt familiar. He'd seen him after the fight with Hank, maybe.

A cruiser pulled into the parking lot. The girl stood and tried to run away. Her leg gave out, and Blue caught her.

"Cry." Blue whispered to her. "Let me do the talking." She gave him a strange look, but wailed convincingly.

"Step away from her." The cop frowned at Blue, hands near his belt.

"Her leg's hurt, officer. I chased away the punk beating her." The remaining bystanders murmured in agreement.

"Fine then, bring her over here and let me have a look at her injuries."

Blue helped the girl to the cruiser, then hoisted her up on the hood. Her t-shirt had been torn exposing a grubby bra and ribs sticking out. Blue slung his jacket around her shoulders, and she pulled it closed.

"Wrong size, but the right colour." Blue said to her.

"Thanks." She hissed when the officer touched her leg, then held her side. Blood ran down her face. The cop handed a gauze dressing to Blue, and he put it up to staunch the flow from a cut over her right eye.

"You should go to the hospital, get that cut stitched up, leg needs looking at too."

"It will get you off the shore for a bit." Blue said quietly. The cop nodded.

"Only if you come with me." The girl shivered. "I trust you, but not him." She nodded at the cop.

Blue's gut twisted. Hospitals were high on his places to avoid list, but something in her eyes tugged at him.

"The ambulance will be here in a few minutes." The cop looked over from where he'd been talking into his mike. Not at all upset that the girl didn't trust him. He wandered over to the crowd and took names, but most of the original bunch had left. Someone came out of the store to talk to him and handed him a bag and a coffee.

"This is for you." The cop looked at the girl but handed them to Blue. "Up to you, but if you eat now, they'll have to wait if any surgery is needed."

The girl paled and swayed. Blue caught her. "Easy."

"What's your name?" The cop had his notebook out.

"Molly."

"Last name?"

Molly sighed and shrank back into the jacket. "Callister."

"Sir?" The officer looked at him expectantly.

"Blue."

"Last name?"

"Just Blue."

The cop snapped his notebook shut. "I'll have someone meet you at the hospital later to take a statement."

Siren's wailing approached quickly, and the vehicle pulled in beside the cruiser.

Blue lifted her from the car onto the stretcher. The paramedics gave her a quick check, then lifted her into the bus.

"Please?" The girl lifted her head to look at Blue. He sighed, unable to turn away from the fear on her face, then jumped in and sat out of the way. They closed the doors, then drove off.

***

Blue bit his cheek as Molly threatened to walk out when the hospital staff didn't want Blue in the room after they learned he wasn't a relation. They gave her gown to replace the torn shirt and jeans.

"I liked your jacket better." She almost smiled at him.

A nurse stitched up the cut, an xray showed no damage to the bones in her leg, but cracks in a couple ribs.

"We'd like to keep you here overnight in case of concussion." The doctor looked at the chart. "I can give you a prescription for painkillers."

"I'm not staying." Molly slid off the bed and would have fallen if Blue hadn't caught her.

"I'll take care of her." Blue wanted to kick himself, but he didn't want to leave this girl alone here, not when he was only barely holding it together himself. It had to be worse for her.

The doctor looked doubtful, but voices on the other side of the curtain interrupted him. Constable Madoc entered the room. The doctor shrugged and left.

Blue hoisted Molly back on the bed and handed her the bag from Timmies and the now cold coffee. She ate the donut in a few bites, then cradled the cup, not looking up at the constable.

"Constable Madoc is one of the good ones." Blue stepped back into the corner.

"Blue." The cop smiled at him. "You doing okay?"

"Well enough."

"Tell me what happened?" Blue told her his story. She made notes with no comments.

"Molly?"

The girl mumbled her way through her story. Constable Madoc's face went from friendly to neutral as she heard about the beating over money the punk said Molly owed him for a fix.

"Can you tell me his name?"

Molly shook her head wildly.

"Okay, if you change your mind." Constable Madoc handed her a card which Molly looked at doubtfully. The gown had no pockets. "I'll see if I can get a set of scrubs for you."

A nurse came in with green scrubs which ballooned out, but covered Molly's body. She put his jacket on over them.

"Can I drop you somewhere?" Constable Madoc asked. "I don't expect you have cab fare."

"Penny Pinchers." Blue said. Molly gave him a look, but the constable didn't blink.

At the thrift shop, Blue left Molly in the hands of a sympathetic woman while he hoofed it over to where he'd stashed his bag. No one was around as he lowered the bag and dug out his card, then headed back to the store.

Molly had changed into black jeans and long-sleeved t-shirt. She held his jacket on her lap, fingers stroking the leather.

"You have any like it in her size?" Blue pointed at the jacket.

The woman disappeared and came back holding two jackets. One was more coat length in dark blue suede. The other was a hot pick motorcycle jacket complete with studs.

Molly waved off the blue one but stared at the pink for a long time. She pulled it on, wincing a bit, then hopped over to the mirror and started laughing until she was holding her side and moaning.

"Oh, it hurts." Molly wiped her face. "I want it."

"It will confuse the hell out of people," Blue said, "but it is bad ass."

He picked up a pair of jeans and two t-shirts for himself, then paid for the clothes and the jacket.

"Let's get something to eat." Blue walked beside Molly ready to help, but while she limped, she refused his support. He picked up tinned food and a few things they could eat that night or didn't need refrigerating.

He led her down to River Trail but sweat beaded her forehead by the time they got there.

"Sit for a bit." He opened up the takeout chicken fingers and potato wedges he'd bought at Safeway. They ate in companionable silence. When the boxes were empty, they started north toward the Halston bridge, then to where he'd stashed his gear.

"I didn't know this was here." Molly looked around. "Sort of quiet."

"Not when the trains come through." Blue laughed, "but you get used to it." He sat back against a tree and patted the ground beside him.

"I don't have anything to pay you with." Molly put her hand on his thigh. "I could manage a freebie…"

Blue put his hand over hers. "Thank you, but no." He leaned his head back and stared up through the leaves. "It's complicated."

"That's all right, you don't need to explain." She sounded more relieved than anything. "I have too many customers and not enough friends." She leaned against him. "Thank you. I wish my father had been like you."

He waited to see if she would say more, but her breath evened out and she slept.

Poor kid, she'd had one hell of a day.

***

Hank tried not to cower as Tad yelled at them. One of the bruisers from the cat house cracked his knuckles.

"There are rumours that ghosts were running about in the park." Tad paced back and forth in front of Hank and the others. "That's exactly the kind of thing you were told could not happen."

"Probably Dan, after all he was stupid enough to get himself dead." One of the others puffed his chest out.

"It happens again, he won't be the only one." Tad got up into the kid's face until he wilted. Hank bit his cheek to keep his nervous giggle in.

"And another thing. Watch for Molly. That bitch owes me. Find her and I'll pay you a C-note." He waved the tan-coloured bill before stuffing it back in his wallet.

Yeah, right. Hank was owed a lot more than a C-note. Tad was a goof, though Hank kept the thought buried deep in his head. Rumour was Tad had killed a guy with his bare hands.

As usual, the others buggered off, leaving Hank alone with the still form of the junkie on his tarp. At least Dan had stuck around, even if he did dick all. The place creeped him out, especially knowing the junkie would probably be a corpse soon.

If only Tad would pay him, he'd be free, and everything would be fine.

CHAPTER 10
Sunday, May 5

Blue woke shivering. He'd wrapped Molly in his sleeping bag while she'd slept. After a train passed by, she'd tossed and turned, crying out in her sleep. Picking her up and cradling her like a child calmed her, now she slept head on his thigh, drooling slightly.

What the hell am I doing? Blue brushed her hair out of her face. She caught his hand and clenched it until his bones ached. He sighed and relaxed his shoulders, trying to breathe like Sam had told him. Maybe it would work again.

The rumble and shriek of a passing train woke her. Molly's eyes went wide, and she recoiled, tangling in the sleeping bag. Blue waited until she calmed, holding her ribs.

"Right, Tad kicked the shit out of me." She fought to sit up. Blue leaned forward to help her, keeping the bag wrapped around her. "You're my angel. Blue, right?"

"That's right." Blue stayed still, just as he would with a strange dog.

"Ugh, I'm all sweaty." She climbed out of the bag and looked at herself in distaste.

"I have spare clothes in the bag." Blue pulled it over to root in it. He tossed them over, along with a bottle of water and a cloth. "Sorry, the shower's broken."

She rolled her eyes, then stripped off her jeans and t-shirt, then underwear, before soaking the cloth and scrubbing herself down. He could count every rib and her arms and legs were stick thin.

"Like what you see?" Molly posed mock provocatively.

61

"I don't think that's a safe question to answer." Blue smiled and caught the cloth she threw at him. He hung it on a bush. She dressed in the wool pants and shirt, running her fingers along the fabric.

"Nice."

Blue dug out a short piece of rope to hold the pants up. She laid the clothes over branches to air out.

"To be honest, the scrubs looked better on you." He stood to untie a rope and lower his food bag. "Peanut butter all right for breakfast?"

They ate half the loaf of bread along with thick gobs of the peanut butter.

"Why was I sleeping with my head on your leg?" Molly sat against a tree; her arms crossed.

"You woke up half in a panic. I rocked you back to sleep. Then you slid down to drool on me." Blue pointed to the damp patch on his jeans.

"Gross." Molly made a face. "I've never met someone who didn't want sex from me. That's why I ended up on the street. Figured I might as well get paid for it."

"I've heard that story a lot." Blue frowned. "My mother worked with an agency that helped girls get off the street."

"Really?" Molly's eyes brightened.

"I haven't talked to mom in over five years. Don't even know if she's alive."

She sagged down in despair. Blue closed his eyes.

"I can look up the agency and see if they're still in business, they were a pretty small one."

"If it's too much..." Molly looked at him through her eyelashes; tears hung from them.

"I can deal with it." Blue packed up the food and hung it back in the tree.

"That's cool."

"Keeps the bears and other things from eating my stash."

"Bears?" Her eyes went wide again.

"Haven't seen any up this way. Had one try to crawl into my sleeping bag with me last year."

"You're joking." She put her hand up to her mouth. "You aren't joking. What did you do?"

"Tried to sleep, if it wanted to kill me it would have. It left by morning."

"So, what's the plan for the day?"

"I think you should stay here." Blue held his breath, but she didn't explode. "Tad will be looking for you. If he sees me around without you, he'll figure you took off."

"You're trusting me not to take off?" Molly's eyes hardened.

"Nothing here can't be replaced." Blue waved a hand. "It would be a nuisance. But it is also not worth much."

"Got you." Molly got up and limped about to spread the sleeping bag out and put her leather jacket on. "Can't believe I'm wearing pink." She ran a hand down the sleeve.

"When you're ready to walk about, it'll confuse the people who will look for black."

Blue stood up and stretched. He counted his change with his fingers. The bank card could stay in his pocket for now.

"If you get hungry, you know where the fridge is."

***

Molly gave him a thumbs up. Blue checked to be sure no one was about, then headed south along Schubert. He'd get coffee at McDonald's. The rest of the day he'd play by ear as long as he was seen alone on Tranquille, it didn't matter.

Sam waved him over to the corner.

"Hear you played the avenging hero yesterday. Was she worth it?"

"She's young enough to be my daughter assuming I had one."

"Would be a turn-on for some."

"Not me." Blue slid out from the table. "Let me grab a coffee, you want a refill?"

"I'm good." Sam slouched back.

Blue returned with his coffee.

"She's not your daughter." Sam leaned on the table.

"No, I give it fifty-fifty odds I'll never see her again."

Sam pulled a phone out of his jacket pocket. "Call someone who can really help her."

Blue took the phone and noted it had already connected to the wifi. He did a search on his mom's agency. It was still around. He pushed the link to phone them before his courage failed him.

"Hello, you've reached..." Blue's heart stopped as he heard his mother's voice and he almost hung up.

"Uh, there's this girl wants help." His words tangled up as the memory of him storming out of the house drunk and screaming obscenities. "Sorry, I'm sorry." Blue disconnected the call before he started blubbering on the phone.

"Breathe." Sam's hand covered his. "There is nothing that can't be survived by taking the next breath."

Blue's guts stopped shaking. He pushed the phone back to Sam.

"Thanks."

"No problem."

Blue sipped at his coffee, still too hot, to buy time to think of an explanation for almost breaking down. But Sam acted like nothing had happened. He put his phone away and played with his empty cup.

"Sam..." Blue ran down.

"When you're ready." Sam put the cup down. "I'll be around."

***

Molly paced about the small camp, trying to work out the stiffness from sleeping on the ground. This Blue, she'd never met anyone like him, and it freaked her out a bit.

Sure, it was nice not to be on her back, but what did he want? Finding out might not be healthy. But if wanted something, why would he walk away and leave his crap for her to steal if she wanted?

She picked up a stick and smacked a tree, but the loud crack made her wince. *Not smart.*

Boredom didn't take long to make itself felt. Molly had been either working, sleeping or taking drugs for the last... she wasn't sure how long it was. Maybe looking around wouldn't be a problem. No sounds came to her other than the hum of cars crossing the Halston Bridge and birds in the trees.

The clothes she wore wouldn't do outside of the camp. They practically screamed homeless and helpless. She needed her black to build her protective shell.

Her own clothes were still damp, but the air was warm enough she didn't worry about them drying. The wool she left spread on the bushes after giving it one more touch with her fingers. That was nicer than anything she'd ever had.

Outside of the little copse of trees she found a park with spruce trees dotted about and a playground in one corner, and there were swings.

Molly sat on a swing and let it drift under her. What was she going to do now? Tad would be after her for sure, but he felt far away in this quiet little park.

An old bald guy with a beard showed up with two dogs and a little boy. The boy ran all over the park, holding the bigger dog's leash. The dog didn't look enthusiastic about it.

"Ronald, stay where I can see you." The old guy leaned on the picnic bench while the smaller dog sniffed around.

The boy ran back and handed the leash over.

"Slide, Poppa."

Did the kid do anything without running? He climbed up and went down the slide a few times, then rode a bumblebee on a spring, back to the slide, back to the bee, then to the swings.

"Push, Poppa!" The old guy lifted Ronald up and made sure he was holding tight, then pushed gently. The kid ran around between the slide, the bee and the swings until Molly couldn't understand why he wasn't falling over from dizziness.

When Ronald dashed over to take the big dog's leash, he waved at Molly, then ran, dragging the dog while his Poppa followed with the small one.

"Wait for me at the gate." The guy nodded at Molly, then followed the kid.

Is that normal? Molly searched her memories. She'd gone to parks as a youngster, even then she'd loved swings, but couldn't recall anyone giving her a push. Certainly no one had followed her around like they had all the time in the world to give her.

She pumped the swing until she reached the point where the chain slackened at the peaks. What did she want? What did Blue want?

The idea of screwing men to pay for drugs so she wouldn't mind screwing them held no interest. The life was a trap, one she'd never figured how to free herself. But the trap had become familiar, mostly predictable, mostly safe.

Molly watched the gravel beneath the swing blur past. Like her life, a blur, no real purpose, no plan.

Freedom terrified her. All her teen years in care she had fought against the system, but as soon as she was free, she'd fallen apart. Maybe she was incapable of living a normal life? She couldn't even imagine it. Trying to put the pieces together felt like one time she'd taken French at school. It disoriented her. The harder she'd worked at it, the more confused she got until even English became hard.

Her feet pointed up into the blue sky, looking like they could vanish into the fluffy clouds

If she took everything, she could sell it and pay Tad enough to get him to back off, at least until the next time. She didn't want to. Not because it was wrong, but because Blue half expected her to do it. He as much as gave her permission. Molly didn't care about disappointing him, she'd been disappointing people her whole life, but her gut clenched at the idea of fulfilling his expectation that she'd rip him off.

Except, did he really assume she'd take his stuff? Gravity pulled at her stomach like the question. *Stay. Go. Stay. Go.* Molly pumped harder, letting the moment of slack, of falling make her heart race.

The decision came on its own out of the blue. Molly let go of the swing and flew through the air, wishing she had wings. Gravity won, as it always did. She landed and rolled laughing until she lay on her back staring up at the sky, hand shading her from the sun.

Molly knew what waited her if she went back. Staying was the risk. Only the faintest glimmer of what might be tickled her mind, but damn she wanted to see it closer, even if it killed her.

***

Blue arrived back at his camp expecting to find it cleared out. Everything was still there, but Molly. She'd changed back into her own clothes and left the wools ones spread out on a bush. He sighed and put the bag he was carrying down. She had to make her own decisions.

The book he'd bought at the dollar store wasn't worth the money he'd spent on it, but it distracted him from acknowledging his disappointment.

"Hi." Molly slipped through the trees. "I was on the swings. Do my best thinking there." She hardly limped at all and sat gracefully beside him and leaned her head on his shoulder. "Did you miss me?"

"Honestly?" Blue restrained his impulse to hug her. "I was worried."

"Really?" She looked up to him, brown eyes shining.

"Really."

Molly snuggled closer, and he gave in and put an arm around her.

"No one's ever worried about me before, worried about money, drugs, sex, but never me." She sighed. "My mom abandoned me as a baby, even my name has nothing to do with her. Grew up in foster homes. Some weren't bad, but as I got older..." She shrugged against him and buried her face in his arm. "The beatings were the least of it, it was the other 'punishments' that made me wild. I'm aged out now. No support, no care."

"Couldn't you get help from the band council?" He spoke without thinking. She gave him a poke in the ribs.

"Didn't you listen? Abandoned, that means no history, no ID, no way to prove anything. I tried." She pointed at her face. "This isn't good enough." She shifted away from him.

Blue couldn't remember what the age limits were for his mom's agency. He'd worked so hard to forget his past, now it frustrated him that it was gone. He'd do more research before he said anything to Molly.

"You're kidding, right?" She held one of the books from the dollar store.

"Better than nothing."

"I guess so." She put the book down. "Was always more into drawing than reading."

"Look in the bag."

69

Molly squealed as she dug out the sketchbook and pencils.

"I used to draw too, so I picked it up."

She squirmed about until she was comfortable, then drew a picture of mushrooms hiding under a bush.

The kid had more talent than he did.

***

"It's your sleeping bag." Molly frowned at him through the evening gloom. Blue held up his hands.

"Not big enough for two. I barely fit, just myself. I'll be fine, I'm used to sleeping cold."

They compromised by leaving the top of the bag unzipped so it could partially cover him. He lay on his leather jacket and wore his wool clothes. His jeans and shirt made a bit of a pillow.

Molly had taken her outer clothes off and pushed them to the bottom of the bag. She lay with her back to him, the heat of her body keeping him awake. He rolled to put his back to hers and blanked his mind.

In the dark of the morning, she half woke and thrashed about. He'd just about made up his mind to wrap her up and rock her to sleep again when she settled, her arms wrapped around his.

Blue stared up into the black of the trees. He had no idea what he was doing, but just like he wasn't about to pull his arm away from her grip, he wasn't going to leave her on her own.

Hope I don't make things worse.

***

Alex McGilvery

Hank arrived back at the cathouse, exhausted from looking everywhere a runaway might hide. The guy who got between her and Tad must have a really well-hidden crash site. The guy had guts. Hank recalled the hard, blue eyes staring into his and his arm twinged. He wouldn't want to face the guy in a real fight. Hell, even Tad backed down.

"Fuck." Tad kicked a chair into a corner of the kitchen. "I can't let a girl do a runner and not punish her."

"Boss told you to keep it quiet, you spot her, just phone her like she said." Nolan leaned against the counter.

"Shit!" Tad kicked another chair, then spotted Hank. "What are you looking at?"

"Saw the guy selling that paper." Hank righted the chair and sank into it. "Maybe he'll do it again. We can follow him."

"You see either of them, you text me." Tad stormed out of the kitchen. Nolan sighed, then looked at Hank.

"Get the hell out of here, kid."

CHAPTER 11
Tuesday, May 7

Blue woke to the screaming of crows. Trains never woke him, but the crows yanked him from sleep every time.

Molly had curled into a ball facing away from him. He slipped out from under the sleeping bag and tucked it in around her, then walked a little way up the track to take care of his morning business, burying it carefully. Smoke and stink were the two surest ways to get a visit from bylaws.

Being alone had never bothered Blue. He happily went days without seeing or talking to anyone. People stressed him, he was sure they expected something, though he never knew what. Selling the paper worked because he knew exactly what he had to do.

He returned to the camp, Molly still slept, looking too young and vulnerable.

By himself, he would have sat still and listened to the birds, content with achieving nothing. Now with Molly a few feet from him, he couldn't relax. Blue settled against one tree, then another. He thought about getting the food down, but that might wake her.

What to do during the day was a problem. At least, he knew what he'd usually do, but that would leave the kid alone all day again. Letting her tag along with him would cause other issues, Tad being the least of them. They could agree to meet back here, but his paranoia about keeping his camps secret wouldn't let him rest. It would be so easy for someone to follow her back. If it had been just him, he'd be moving to a different spot tonight, or tomorrow night at the latest. He'd talk to Molly about it; or should he just say they were moving? The other places weren't as close to a park or swings.

Molly woke and stretched. She grinned at him before crawling out of the bag and getting dressed. While modesty would be a luxury in these circumstances, Blue couldn't help but wonder how she could be so casual with someone she'd only met a few days ago.

"Good morning." She came back from her visit to the woods. "Did I drool on you last night?"

"Nope, no drool." Blue lowered his food bag and dug into it. "You want peanut butter again, or granola bars?"

"Peanut butter." Molly rubbed her stomach. "Granola bars just don't do it for me."

They ate, sharing the last bottle of water.

"What are we doing today?"

"I have sort of a routine, depending on the change in my pockets. Coffee at McDonald's, wander around, chat with people here and there most of the day, come back, move camp, eat something cold out of a tin."

"Sounds boring." Molly wrapped her arms around her legs.

"It is. Excitement is trouble."

"I usually slept all day, then worked..." She reddened and put her head down.

"You did what you had to." Blue sighed. "Don't be ashamed of surviving. The thing is, when you get a choice, you'll have to make it. I'm not going to tell you how to live, though I will admit I have opinions on the subject."

"Opinions?" Molly lifted her head.

"Opinions." Blue fluttered his hand. "As in ideas unsupported by any fact or experience."

"Let's hear these opinions." Her voice had hardened, and she frowned at him.

Stupid. No getting out of this hole in one piece.

"I think you should have the choice—to be in the trade if you want, to not be in it if you want. We, our society, are not very good at allowing either. We tell girls, women, boys, whoever, it is a terrible thing, but what do we offer in its place?"

"You think I *chose* to make a living hooking?" She stood up and paced in the tiny clearing, arms wrapped tight around her.

"No, I expect you ended up in a place you didn't think you had any other way to survive, which is why I will never blame you or think badly of you because of that."

"You don't?" Molly stared at him through tears.

"I..." Blue put his hand to his head. "Give me a second, I don't want to screw this up." He breathed slowly until the buzz in his chest subsided a little. "Mom brought home a girl, don't remember why. But this kid spent the entire hour swearing at me, blaming me for all her problems while mom did whatever she needed to do. I probably didn't help matters by arguing it was her own problem. Later, mom told me the girl had never been allowed to make her own decisions since she was recruited off the street. Other people dictated everything, from what men she saw, to the clothes her wore, even the drugs her took."

Molly nodded.

"First thing she decided for herself was to get out. Then she had to decide everything. Who she wanted to be, what she wanted to be, where she wanted to go. It was overwhelming. So, she could retreat into fear and go back, or get angry and use that to move forward." Blue's gut churned. *Who am I to talk?*

"I don't get it, what does that do with not blaming me?"

"You are who you are, not what you did. I saw that kid as what she did, and she probably felt it. That took away her decision to change. I swore I'd never fall into that trap again." Blue sighed and smacked his forehead. "I suck at explaining this stuff."

"My decision." Molly's pacing slowed. "If I said I was going back to work, you wouldn't stop me."

"No, I wouldn't." Blue rubbed his gut. "That doesn't mean I wouldn't care, but I don't have the right to stop you from living your own life."

"You care about me?" She looked poised to run in panic.

"We're friends." Blue held her gaze.

"Friends." Molly shook her head. "I've never had friends. I don't know how."

"This." Blue waved at the space between them. "We've eaten together, shared a camp, talked about scary stuff."

"Scary?" She raised her eyebrows.

"I've been less scared with a gun pointed at me."

Her mouth dropped open, and she came toward him like he might flee at any second, then dropped to sit beside him and wrapped his arm around her shoulders like a blanket.

"I hate guns." She leaned her head against him. "I take all my clothes off, and you don't tell me to get dressed. I'm dressed and you aren't trying to get my clothes off. I don't understand you at all. No one has ever touched me without wanting sex, but here you are, I can sit with you and not need to do anything." Her head twisted around to look at him. "What if *I* wanted sex?"

"Sorry, sex is a game for two, and I'm not in the game."

"Weird." Molly relaxed and sighed. "But I can live with it."

"Thanks, kid."

The crows settled their daily argument and flew off. The air grew warmer. Blue thought the girl had gone to sleep when she sat bolt upright.

"Let's go for a hike."

"A hike?"

"Yeah, just go somewhere no one is around."

"I think a hike could work."

***

Blue carried Molly into the camp and set her down as the light was fading.

"I didn't think walking would be so much work." She kicked off her shoes and rubbed her feet. "Better shoes would help."

"You did well." Blue stretched the kinks out of his back. "I only needed to carry you the last bit."

"I'm surprised those people weren't calling the police on us."

"We acted like people out enjoying the day, why would they be suspicious?"

"I guess." Molly retrieved the food bag pulling out tins without looking at the labels. "Supper time."

CHAPTER 12

"I'll stay here and rest." Molly rubbed her legs. "I can't remember ever walking that far before."

"Okay, you know where the fridge is."

"That's it? You aren't going to tell me to be careful?"

"Do I need to?"

"No," Molly's face burned. "But it would be nice."

Blue smiled and wrapped his arms around her. "Be careful."

His arms made her feel safe. She imagined this was what a father should feel like. He let her go and walked out of the camp without looking back.

With them going on the walk yesterday, they were getting low on water. Maybe Blue would pick some up or knew where they could refill their bottles.

Was this what normal life was like? Worrying about water, and mundane things, not about whether the next guy would want it rough, or try to rob her?

The men in her life growing up didn't act like fathers. Either they felt her up or beat her down. None of the men since had been different.

"Don't go there." Molly smacked her leg and zipped up her jacket to the collar, then pulled out the sketchbook and pencils. She drew the surrounding trees. Then sat under the railway bridge to draw the ducks.

The ducks morphed from the busy, squabbling flock into dark predators with slitted eyes and fangs. The bridge twisted into something out of a horror movie. People with dead eyes walked decaying dogs along a broken path.

When she couldn't stand it anymore, she dropped the stuff in the camp and went to sit on the swing. She swung higher and harder until her sobs made it impossible to hang on. The gravel under the swing bit into her palms and knees and scratched her face. Molly welcomed the pain. She deserved it.

Before, she would have begged a hit from Tad, putting her deeper into his debt, and all the agony would float away. But she'd left all that behind. Hadn't she?

Who was she kidding? Get off the street, get a real life? Blue lived out of a pack hung in a tree. The only reason he wasn't banging her was his weirdness. At some point, he'd want something from her. Why else would he be doing all this?

"Are you injured?" A man's voice spoke next to her. She'd curled into a fetal position. Instead of answering, she pulled in tighter. If she willed it hard enough, her heart would stop. It had never worked, but it didn't stop her from trying.

"Doesn't seem to be intoxicated." The man talked to someone Molly couldn't hear.

"Is she all right?" An older woman's voice made her shudder. Some old people were the worst.

"We've called Car 40, they'll be able to assess her and get her the help she needs."

"Car 40?"

"They work with mental health cases."

"That's sounds like a good idea."

Mental health? Was she crazy? She didn't feel crazy, just... broken.

"Hey," a new woman's voice sounded familiar. "When you're ready to talk, I'm here."

Even with just touching, the woman's presence eased something in Molly's chest. She straightened out, lying on her back with her eyes closed.

"Molly, right?" The woman didn't sound surprised.

Molly opened her eyes and rubbed the tears out of them. "You were at the hospital."

"You went through a rough time; it isn't surprising for it to hit you later." Constable Madoc knelt beside her.

Molly snorted. "He's beat me worse."

"I don't doubt it, but you're a tough woman."

"I don't want to be tough." Molly wailed.

"I can understand that."

Molly sat up and peered at her knees where they peeked bloodily through tears in the denim.

"Look at these jeans, and Blue just got them for me." She hugged her knees and rocked. "He's going to be so mad."

"Maybe, maybe not." The cop shrugged. "He's got a lot buried inside, but he doesn't seem the type to get angry about something like that."

"He's the first nice man I've ever met." Molly's chest burned with the need to defend him.

"Then I expect he'll be more worried about your wounds than the jeans."

"I guess." Exhaustion hit her.

"How about you let these people clean you up? Then you can decide what's next."

"Me decide?"

"Why not?"

Molly held out her hands. The paramedic took them and cleaned the gouges, then did her knees and cheek.

"All good here?"

"Thank you." Molly whispered, but the man was looking at Constable Madoc, who nodded.

"Want to talk here, or should we go get something to eat?"

"Food would be nice."

The cop stood, then offered a hand to Molly and hoisted her up. "Come on, I'll introduce you to my partner."

John was quiet, but his eyes observed everything. She put her hand to her hair, greasier than she ever let it get. Showers weren't worth going back to that life. They parked at Wendy's and the three of them walked in, getting more than a few stares.

"I need to use the washroom."

"What do you want to eat? I'll order for you." Constable Madoc didn't offer to accompany her, nor appear worried that Molly would disappear.

"Burger, fries, coke. Whatever."

In the washroom Molly soaked her hair and tried to use the soap to wash it. By the time she was done, her t-shirt was drenched, but strangely, she felt better. Molly put her pick jacket back on.

Out in the restaurant, the cop waved at her from a corner.

"John will bring the food over." She didn't ask about the water dripping from Molly's hair or the t-shirt stuck to her skin under her jacket.

"You want to talk about it?"

"About what?" Molly's palms went sweaty.

"Why you were crying in the playground. The woman got worried and called to report it."

"Blue and I talked about life." Molly rolled her eyes. "That sounds so lame."

"You want to tell me about it?"

"Not really." Her face burned, and she covered it with her hands.

"Fair enough."

John arrived with the food, and they dug in. Constable Madoc's radio crackled occasionally, but she didn't respond to it.

"I'll give you my card again." She slid it across to Molly. "If you need to talk, call me. I'm a regular cop, so I get busy, but I will get back to you when I can."

"Here's some information for you. Look at it later." John put a brochure on the table. "It lists supports you can access. Unfortunately, none of it will be fast, but it doesn't hurt to get started."

Molly took the brochure and card reluctantly and put them in her back pocket.

A shiver run down her spine and she looked around the restaurant, but nobody was paying them the slightest attention.

"What?" Constable Madoc scanned the crowd.

"I felt like someone was watching me," Molly said, "must just be creeped out."

"You need a ride somewhere?"

"No, I'm looking for new jeans and maybe better shoes."

"I'll keep an eye out while you cross the street."

"I'm not a kid." Molly spoke louder than she intended, then looked down.

"No, you're not." John's expression made her squirm, though he had a slight smile. "But she's a cop." He shrugged.

"Does she watch you cross the street?" Molly asked.

"Nope, I tell him when he's drunk too much coffee."

Molly and John shared a grin, and a knot in her gut loosened.

"Be careful." Constable Madoc stood and took the tray with the garbage.

"You too." Molly's nerves came back soon as she was out the door, though no one was around but a couple families with kids. She crossed over to the Penny Pincher and went through the jeans, but nothing she liked was in her size. The shoes weren't any better.

"There's another thrift shop that way, in the old SPCA building. The woman at the counter pointed north along Eighth."

Molly found the cute little shop. They had a pair of boots in her size that called her name.

"Sorry we can't hold anything." The woman at the counter said.

"I guess." Molly looked longingly at the black boots. "I'll come back again."

She wandered out of the store and scanned the street. Nothing.

I don't want to ask Blue for more money. The only way she knew to make money turned her stomach. She'd never willingly go back to that life. There had to be another way.

CHAPTER 13

Blue had been on edge all day. Sam hadn't been at the McDonald's. He bought a t-shirt for Molly on impulse at a thrift shop, then felt self-conscious carrying the bag with him.

It might have been only the bag making him uneasy, but the back of his neck prickled. That wasn't a sensation he'd felt in years. His hands wanted to shake, and he didn't trust his knees. A family walking along the street, mother, father and two kids turned his gut to jelly.

Blue leaned against the wall of a storefront to keep from collapsing on the sidewalk.

The kids, excited to be eating out, ran about the restaurant while the father ordered the meals. His eyes glowed red and blood dripped from his hands.

He wouldn't go there. What would Molly do if he fell apart here?

"Want to come in and sit down?" A professional-looking woman stood holding a door open. "We're Ask Wellness, but you're welcome to rest a bit." Blue followed her into the place and sat gratefully.

"Water?" the woman asked.

"Thanks, but no." Blue leaned his head back. "Just a bit shaky."

"Well then, shout out if you need something." She disappeared through a door. People came in and out. Some had appointments, others needed forms. Brochures were placed strategically around the room advertising programs for mental health, addictions and more. Blue pushed himself to his feet. The weakness had vanished as quickly as it hit.

Outside, a bunch of teens bunched up on the far side of the street. One of them might have been Hank. As he walked north, some of the teens split off and headed north on the far side of the street.

Stopping to look in the window of a shop, Blue watched the reflection of his shadows. Sure enough, they went to loitering mode. He entered the shop, Lo-boy Market and wandered the aisles. He bought a few tins of stuff, then went back out and north again, stopping in at every store and spending varying times inside before moving along. By the time he'd reached Subway only a couple of his followers remained. He bought two sandwiches, then crossed the street to the Mall and went into the Independent. They were getting low on peanut butter and he picked up more bread, some fruit from the fifty percent off rack, and a jug of water.

The boys followed him at a distance through the store, looking bored. A security guard approached them, and they headed the other way. Probably out of habit. Blue paid for his few groceries at the customer service counter, then walked through the Mall out past the busses and headed toward Schubert. He saw no sign of his tail while waiting for the lights, but still zigzagged through the streets so he wasn't visible from a distance.

Only dog walkers occupied the path, then Blue took the first path down the bank. Even if they searched Schubert, they'd have a hard time finding him. At the

Halston Bridge he climbed back onto the path, but there was no one in any direction.

In a few minutes he was back at camp. Molly wasn't there.

She was probably on the swings. The drawing book lay in the clearing like she'd thrown it in. *Odd, the girl had been very protective of the thing.* He picked it up to put in a safer spot, then thumbed through to see what she'd added. The new drawings started normally enough, but page by page they twisted into something that made his skin crawl.

The darkness and despair in the art called to him. He'd been in that place more than once. Blue put the book down carefully, packed the food into the food sac and hoisted it up.

He started looking for her by walking along the trail past the park. She wasn't on the swings. Next he checked the trees, some of the spruce might make hiding places, uncomfortable, but effective.

An older woman came out of a house across the street.

"You looking for your daughter?" She called out. He crossed over to her.

"You've seen her?"

"She fell off the swings this morning and wasn't moving. I called the ambulance, but she must have been fine since she went off with the police. A woman constable and a man in street clothes."

"Thank you." Blue didn't know whether to be relieved or more worried.

The woman looked around and lowered her voice. "I know you are camping near here." She lifted a hand. "I won't say a thing, my son lived on the street for a while. If the girl is in trouble again, tell her to knock on my door and I'll call for whatever help she needs."

"Thank you." Blue looked at the house number. *We all have our stories.*

She went back into her house and Blue wandered about more before slipping into the camp. Only three days, and now it felt empty without her.

He sat against his usual tree and contemplated the possibilities.

One. They'd arrested her, though from what the woman said, she looked more injured than misbehaving. Unless there was a warrant, but nothing had been mentioned when they were at the hospital.

A second. They took her up to the hospital for assessment. If that was the case, Molly might or might not get out until late. Mental health never seemed to count as an emergency.

There might be something in between. Getting more information about the assault or some other thing. Madoc said Car 40 was assigned to mental health situations. There were plenty of agencies they might take her to.

Last was they'd talked, dropped her off, and she'd left. It would be strange for her to leave the sketchbook behind, but there was nothing else she owned here.

His mind went round and round like a hamster on a wheel, imagining worse and worse things.

Breathe.

Blue put his head on his knees and focused on his breathing, letting it wash away the thoughts and images that tried to change into the red room. He used his breath as a shield until nothing existed but the movement of air in out of his lungs.

"Blue?" A hand rested on his shoulder. "Blue are you okay? You're scaring me."

He lifted his head and blinked tears from his eyes. Molly knelt beside him.

"You too?"

Blue nodded, not willing to trust his voice. She wrapped her arms around him and put her head on his chest. "I'm sorry I wasn't here."

"You're here now." His voice rasped, but her warmth made a better shield from the darkness than just his breathing. He closed his eyes again and relaxed.

"I broke down on the swings and fell off. Someone called the ambulance; they called the cops. That woman cop, Madoc came with John, her partner. They're actually pretty cool for being cops. We ate at Wendy's then I looked through some thrift shops. I had this weird feeling, so I walked west on Halston before doubling back here."

"Good, always trust those instincts." Blue gave her a squeeze. "I had a bunch of kids following me. I bored them to death, then let Mall security deal with them."

"Tad." Molly shivered and Blue tightened his hold. "He will want me back. If I make the break, the other girls might, and he won't risk that."

"We could leave town." Blue said. "I like it here, but there isn't much keeping me here."

Molly shook her head.

"Okay. I bought subs. There're in the food bag. Fighting the darkness makes me hungry, how about you?"

She laughed and fetched the bag down, dug out the sandwiches and found the bag with the shirt. "You bought this?"

"It made me think of you."

Molly put the shirt up to her face and breathed in, then took her jacket and shirt off and put the new one on. It was black, but silver paint outlined a skull with fangs like a vampire.

"How does it look?"

"Great."

She put the jacket back on, then held up the Subway bag. "Which do you want?"

"Either is good."

Molly opened one and handed him half a sandwich. They ate both, then sat back and sighed in unison. Molly giggled.

"I saw these wicked jeans and boots..."

Blue noticed the tears in the knees, and the scratches on her face and winced. "How much are they asking?"

"Both together would be twenty." Molly held up her hands. "You are not paying for them."

"It's early enough in the month you could make that selling papers."

"That Big Edition thing?"

"That would be it. You can sell on the North Shore or go over to Downtown."

"I'm not allowed across the bridge." Molly said, then frowned. "Tad's territory is the North Shore, some other guy runs the south. He won't know I've run away."

"North Shore it is. As long as you're on Tranquille, he won't likely try anything. I'll keep an eye out."

"I don't want you standing around like a worried father."

"You won't see me. I won't interfere unless it gets dangerous."

"Promise?"

"Promise." Blue put his hand on his heart.

CHAPTER 14
Wednesday, May 8

They approached Tranquille from the south end. Blue walked under the Overlander for the first time since finding Rooster's body. He carefully kept his eyes in front. He led Molly to The Big Edition office and turned her over to Dabra for orientation.

Over in The Loop section, Blue left his leather jacket in Jake's keeping and picked up a worn hoody from the table of clothes. A camo baseball cap shaded his face. From the lack of skill shown by his shadows the day before, it would probably be enough. He bummed a cigarette and stood with the thing burning slowly to ash until Molly left the building carrying a bag filled with newspapers.

She walked slowly north on the west side of the street. He meandered along behind her; just another bum. A few people stopped and bought papers. Some boys stopped her to pose and try to prove their cool factor. From the red ears, Blue suspected she'd put them in their place.

A woman bumped into Molly. Molly kept her feet, but the woman crashed to the sidewalk. Movement caught Blue's attention as someone in a shiny leather jacket sauntered away, hands in his pockets. The right size to be Tad, but Blue couldn't be sure.

Meanwhile, Molly had helped the other woman up, she was strung out, thin and underdressed for the spring weather. It took a moment for Blue to recognize Hannah. So, this was the new place she'd found. He frowned in sympathy. It was far too easy to manipulate desperate people. Molly was his concern today. Maybe if they did something about Tad, she'd be able to break free too.

Molly walked along the street while Hannah went back toward the alley, as if she'd only come to bump into Molly. Blue ran over reasons the woman might want to contact Molly. Did they even know each other? Maybe the issue was what Tad wanted.

Molly crumpled a piece of paper and dropped it on the sidewalk. Blue scooped it up. A tiny package hid in the paper. He slipped that into his pocket and dropped the paper in the trash. Up ahead a police car pulled up beside her and a cop climbed out calling to Molly. She glared at the officer.

Keep your cool.

Blue got close enough to hear their conversation and stopped to tie his shoe, keeping his head down.

"...reported someone with a Big E bag was selling drugs."

"So you rushed over and stopped the first person you saw with a bag?" Molly wasn't hiding her sarcasm.

"They gave a description." The cop frowned, and his fingers tapped his belt.

Molly lifted the papers out of the bag and handed them to the cop, then turned the bag inside out.

"You going to check them or not?" Molly pointed at the stack in the cop's hand. He riffled through each paper, then handed it back to Molly, who put it into her bag. A crowd had gathered around, watching and commenting. Blue recognized a couple of Hank's hangers-on.

Next Molly emptied her pockets into the cop's hands. He struggled to hold on to the change and bills.

"Don't drop it, I worked hard for that." She turned her pockets inside out. Then put her hands out for the cop to return her money. He eyed it suspiciously before giving it back.

"You could have it hidden somewhere else." His face red, the cop had a stubborn look to him.

"If you are going to charge her, then do so, otherwise move on." A woman in an expensive suit stepped forward and stared at the officer expressionlessly.

"Fine." He stomped around to get in his car and drove away.

"That must have been a trial, dear," the woman's face softened into sympathy.

"Nah, I've dealt with him before." Molly grinned at the woman. "He looks tough, but he's a stickler for the rules. Must be gay, he's never tried to get any freebies from me when I was in the business."

The woman's face darkened.

"Perhaps we should talk more in my office." She pointed to the storefront with a sign advertising legal services. *Was that there before?* Blue couldn't recall. At second look the woman wasn't very old, and could be just trying to drum up business, though Molly was hardly an ideal client.

"Sorry, I haven't made enough yet." Molly looked around. "Anyone want to buy a Big Edition?" A few people purchased papers, including the woman in the suit. Molly continued north, Blue crossed the street with a few others.

The woman went into the office and didn't come back out. He'd better catch up to Molly.

After she'd reached the Salvation Army building, she crossed the street and worked her way south to the office and went in to return the bag. Blue ducked into The Loop to retrieve his jacket and put the hoody and hat back on the table. He met Molly outside.

"How did you do?"

"What, you didn't count my take when the cop was holding it?" Molly smirked at him. "I recognized your boots."

"I'm impressed." Blue grinned back at her. "What was that about?"

"You picked up the paper, right?" Molly looked worried.

"I did, was that what the cop was expecting to find?"

"That woman put something in my pocket when she knocked into me. I felt it when I went to give her a bit of change. Couldn't get rid of it fast enough."

"Smart thinking." Blue headed south, they crossed under the bridge and he walked onto the trails crossing through the trees.

Only when he was sure they were alone did he pull the thing from his pocket. It was a tiny plastic zip bag holding white powder.

"Shit, if he'd found that..." Molly was pale.

"Enough to take you in, but not to charge you with trafficking." Blue peered at it closer, then opened it to dump it on the ground. He spread it around with his toe until no trace of white remained. The bag he buried, then brushed grass and leaves over it. "In the future, don't voluntarily allow a search. Even if you are sure it will clear you. Not every cop plays by the rules."

"Yes, sir." Molly saluted him, then stuck her tongue out.

"Sorry, old habit."

"Giving advice or thinking like a cop?" Molly crossed her arms and challenged him, chin up.

"Bit of both." Blue pushed back the buzz in his chest and met her eyes.

"Right." Molly patted her pocket. "I want to get to the thrift shop before it closes, so let's hoof it."

"As you wish." Blue sighed and followed her.

***

Hank leaned against a tree. Waiting on Schubert had paid off. The old guy and the girl had strolled passed his hiding spot. They disappeared by the park. Only one place they could be crashing. He pulled out his phone and texted Tad.

Maybe the jerk would cough up some cash. The phone was almost out of minutes. Hank added it to the ever-growing amount of money owed him for being part of this shit show.

***

Molly paraded about the campsite in her new jeans and boots. They'd even been able to get her new underwear at the Independent.

Blue tried to figure out what benefit Tad thought to get from setting the police on Molly. He had a hard time connecting a woman lawyer with a pimp and drug dealer. She had too much to lose. Molly thought that cop was straight-laced, but it wouldn't be the first time a cop had turned.

"What gives?" Molly plunked herself down beside Blue. "You have this serious as shit face that's creeping me out."

"Sorry." Blue shook his head and tried to put his worries aside. Molly waggled her finger. "If you're worrying about me, I want to hear it."

"I spotted someone who might have been Tad when the woman bumped into you. I'm trying to figure what he'd get out of a cop harassing you."

"He's probably got friends in lock-up." Molly shrugged. "Figured to have them rough me up and give me a warning. But that suit interrupted, Tad's probably furious right now."

"Lawyers don't usually interrupt the police in their work. Movies aside, lawyers aren't about solving crime."

"Are you undercover?" Molly swivelled to look at him.

"No." Red images flashed behind his eyes. Blood ran from an open wound in her neck. Dolls bled onto wood floors. A man with half a head slumped under the window. Something shook him, garbled words splashed against his ears. He put his hands up to shut them out. Darkness offered a way out of the red room, so he dove into it.

***

He came to with his head on something soft. Warm drops splashed on his face.

"Blue?" Molly's voice broke. "Blue, I don't know what to do."

He opened his eyes to look up into her tear-stained face.

"Sorry."

"You were mumbling about blood and dead people." She brushed his hair back from his face, then used her t-shirt to wipe her tears away.

"I can't talk about it without going back." Blue tried to sit up but had no strength.

"It's okay, I'm sorry."

"Don't be sorry." Blue stared up into her glistening eyes. "It isn't your fault."

"But..."

Blue put a finger over her lips. "I'm sorry for scaring you."

"I almost kept that baggie." Molly bent her head until he couldn't see her face through her hair. "That's how I survived. The drugs made it all not matter, only the high. Then I thought you'd be disappointed, so I dumped it, hoping someone would put it in the trash. I about died when you picked it up. Without you, I'd be high and screwing some john."

"You're stronger than you think." He reached up and ran his fingers across her cheek. "You made all the choices to get here."

"I forgot I had these in my pocket until I changed my jeans." Molly held a card and brochure.

A snap alerted Blue. "Hide."

Molly looked at him, eyes wide.

"Quick, run, hide. Get to that woman's house." Blue rolled to his feet to face whoever was coming. Behind him

Molly screamed, and he spun to see Tad holding her around the waist as she flailed wildly. Burning pain made him grunt, then a kick sent him to the ground. Boots hammered at him while he tried to curl up and protect his head. Molly had gone quiet. *That's bad, get up.*

Instead, a kick landed on his head.

***

The room was white with the unique smell of a hospital. Blue's first reaction was disappointment. Not waking up would have been so much easier. Then he thought of Molly and tried to sit up. Pain lanced across his back.

"Lie quiet a bit longer," a nurse's professional tones made him stop, if not relax.

"How long was I out?"

"I don't know when they brought you in, but it is past midnight." The nurse came over and checked his pulse, then his blood pressure.

"Damn, can you call the police? I need to talk to them."

"Funny, they'd like to talk to you too." She tutted at something, then re-arranged the blanket over him slightly. "If you're up to it, I can let them know you're awake."

Blue didn't know the officers who came into the room. He couldn't help the tension that gripped his gut and made his mouth dry.

"What did you want to tell us?" the shorter officer said, his notebook already out, pen poised.

"The clearing where I was found." Blue barely croaked out the words. "There was a girl camping with me. About 160 cm, 45 kg, very slim build, black hair, brown eyes, maybe 19 years old, dressed in black, but wearing a bright pink leather jacket and black ankle boots. Looks First Nations."

The officer wrote down the description, then nodded to his partner; she went out into the hall, already putting her hand to her radio mic.

"What is your relationship with this girl?"

"Her name is Molly, maybe last name Callister. We are friends."

"Friends." The officer wrote, keeping his face blank.

"Whoever attacked me took her..." Blue gasped for air, then explained about Tad, the first assault and the stop on the street, only leaving out the bag with the drugs.

"My partner has alerted everyone. They'll be on the lookout for her." He shifted slightly. "How long have you been 'camping' with this girl?"

"Just a few days." Blue stared at the ceiling.

"You said she was nineteen, but perhaps she was younger? Maybe fourteen or fifteen?"

"Anonymous tip?" Blue's lips quirked. "Molly said she'd aged out of the foster care system and that's how she ended up hooking. She might have lied, but I don't think so."

"Right." The officer put his notepad away. "First thing is to find the girl. You stay here and rest."

As soon as the door closed behind the cop, Blue dragged himself out of bed. He found his clothes and slipped out of the room. Molly was out there.

CHAPTER 15
Thursday, May 9

Molly groaned. The sound-proofed room was all too familiar. She'd not always been an obedient girl, and this was where Tad disciplined any who didn't dance to his tune.

Her clothes lay in a pile in the corner, deliberately just out of reach from the bed. Once she'd proven suitably punished, she'd be allowed to dress, then return to work. The pink jacket was missing, but that wasn't a surprise. It was a rebellion against the image Tad crafted her into.

The familiar cuffs fastened her right arm to the bed. They were tight enough on her wrist to guarantee she couldn't slip out. She expected they were fastened to the usual bar on the cast iron bed frame.

Her head ached, and her vision blurred. They would leave her here until she was tired and thirsty and the pot under the bed stunk from her own shit. Tad followed the same playbook each time. Molly assumed he'd do the same this time. At least she was alive.

The tiny red light glowed in the corner. The other girls whispered rumours that it fed to a tv screen where the guys could watch and get off on the girl's punishment. She expected it recorded footage to make porn videos, after all, sex and violence were big sellers.

Molly sat and turned her back to the camera. If it was a live feed, they'd get bored with her bony back quickly enough. The other cuff hooked through a loop in the iron. A crack ran almost all the way through the loop. How many had screamed and fought to make that crack?

Both hands gripping the cuff on her wrist, Molly planted her feet against the cast iron headboard and heaved. Did it creak? She redoubled her efforts, expected Tad or one of his goons to break in a beat her bloody.

Her back and legs screamed in agony from the strain, but the crack looked to be growing.

It gave with a snap, sending her tumbling backwards off the bed to lie in a heap, gasping for air.

I don't have time for this. Molly crawled over to the clothes and dressed as fast as she could make her weak arms and legs move.

A faint creak was her only warning the door was opening. She plastered herself against the wall.

The first person through the door was Tad, and one of his bruisers followed close on his heels. Tad turned to scan the room and opened his mouth to shout. Molly kicked the bruiser between the legs, then pushed him into Tad. She jumped through the door and pulled it shut, dropping the bar before Tad could get his fingers in place to pull it open.

The hall had other doors leading to rooms where the girls would do drugs and sleep until it was time to sell themselves again. At the end of the hall was a small window, stairs went down to the right. Behind her would be a blank wall separating the two parts of the building.

She ran to the window. Experience told her it would only lift a few inches, just enough to let air into the hall. Holding the loose cuff like brass knuckles, Molly punched the window. Glass flew all over. Feet pounded downstairs. She scraped the jagged edges of the glass away from the frame, then dove through. Pain told her she hadn't cleared it away well enough.

"Go outside and see what's up."

That was Nolan. Molly stood on the peaked roof of the entry. She didn't think she could outrun any of the guys. Blue's gear bag hanging in the tree came to mind. After a mad scramble, Molly rolled onto the flat roof of the side-by-side. She could try lowering herself to one of the other entries, but as far as she knew, Tad owned the entire building.

A tree stood by one corner, the only green thing surrounded by bare dirt and cement. Back in the day she'd stared out the window more than once imagining climbing the tree like Jack's beanstalk and escaping the world. It would have to wait.

Yelling outside cut off at a shout from Tad.

"She can't have gone far. Do a sweep, keep it down, we don't want the cops showing up."

"Should have just offed her." Nolan growled.

"Even if she makes it to the cops, we do what we always do. Get one of the girls ready to play the part. Without a warrant, they can't do squat."

"Don't like it."

"You don't need to like it." Tad said. "We get her back, then she goes to the coast with the next bunch. She'll think this was heaven when they get done with her."

"What about the other thing?"

"What about it? It hits the streets the long weekend like we planned." Tad sounded strange, nervous. "Or do you want to explain the delay to the Boss?"

"Not me, that one makes my balls shrink."

Tad must have gone back inside. The door slammed, shaking the whole building.

A cop car swung by, Molly thought about standing up and waving, but they passed before she gathered the nerve. The air grew chillier, and she rubbed her arms to stay warm. The lights below went out.

The tree wasn't as close to the roof as it looked from below. On her tiptoes, her fingers brushed the closest branch. It should hold her weight. When she jumped and caught it, it creaked but held her feet dangling just above the roof.

"Just like when I was a kid." Molly breathed in deep, then went hand over hand along the branch toward the tree. Her arms shook by the time she reached the point where she could get her feet on a branch below. From there she climbed down the far side, then limped away. She had to check on Blue. If they'd killed him...

It felt like hours later when she arrived at the railway bridge. *What if someone had stayed behind?* She felt her way along the trail to the camp, praying she wouldn't find Blue cold and dead.

A hand covered her mouth. "Molly, it's me."

She went weak, and he had to hold her up.

"There's two of them watching. I came back to get my gear and got lucky, heard them talking before they heard me." He led her back under the bridge. "I think we need to go to ground somewhere safe. Sam's not too far from here."

She hobbled along, holding his hand, hissing through her teeth. Now that the frantic fear over Blue faded, the pain took its place.

Blue scratched an old blue tent with a long stick.

"Sam, it's Blue. I need your help."

After an eternity, a light went on in the tent.

"This had better be good." A voice growled, and Molly shivered.

"Come on," Blue led her into the campsite.

Molly giggled as Santa Claus crawled out of the tent wearing sweat pant and a torn grey t-shirt.

"You must be Molly." Sam looked at her and his eyes widened. He backed into the tent to come out with a box. "If you're here, you won't be convinced to go to the hospital." He opened the box and took out gauze and tape. "You're not the first to come to me for first aid."

"You aren't a normal street person." Blue held the flashlight so Sam could see to work.

"Are you?" Sam didn't look up from his work. Most of the cuts were shallow and had already stopped bleeding. One oozed blood, and Molly bit back a scream when he poked at it. "Really needs stitches." He fished tweezers out of the box, then gave her a roll of cloth. "Bite on this."

Fortunately, he found and extracted the chunk of glass, so pressure on the cut no longer caused agony. After taping gauze over the wound, he pointed to the tent. "I'm old enough to be chivalrous by instinct. Go lie down and sleep. It's clean enough."

Molly didn't need a second invitation.

CHAPTER 16
Friday, May 10

Every part of Molly's body ached. She grumbled as she chewed on the granola bar. Shoved the sleeve of the sweatshirt Sam loaned her up her wrist again.

"We need to get Molly out of town." Blue rubbed his back and winced. "Out of reach of Tad and his gang."

"No." Molly wanted to stomp around and break things. Fat lot of good that would do. "I don't want to run away, and what about you? Will you leave town too?"

"I'm planning on wandering into the back country for a while." Blue's forehead wrinkled. "It's a different thing than hanging out beside a park."

"And you're saying I can't handle it?" Molly jumped to her feet and almost collapsed at his feet. Sam caught her arm and steadied her.

"Keep it down. The dog-walkers will pretend they don't know we're here, but if it sounds like a fight, the cops will be here before you know it."

"Sorry." Molly sat down and put her head on her knees to hide the tears.

"You're both hurt, not the best time to be planning major changes." He put a hand on her shoulder. Molly shrugged it off.

"Don't touch me."

"Molly—"

"It's all right, Blue. She has the right." Sam didn't sound at all upset. "Let's leave the long-term thinking for a moment. I don't have enough to feed you and me, not to mention only having one spoon. I'm going to go do a bit of shopping. While I'm gone, don't make any noise. Talk about something safe, let yourselves cool down."

His footsteps receded. Birds chirped and flitted in the trees. A train whistle blew, and the sound cracked her heart. Sobs wracked her body. She wanted Blue to hold her, but he wouldn't, not after she blew off Sam.

"Molly," Blue sounded hesitant. "Anything I can do to help?"

Her heart wanted to crawl into his lap and cry like a baby. Her mind mocked her weakness. Her body refused to move.

"Hold." The word came as a whisper barely audible even to her own ears, but strong arms lifted her, rocked her.

The crying fit passed, and Molly relaxed, leaning her head against Blue's chest.

"Better?" Blue gave her a slight squeeze.

She nodded, not ready to trust her voice. His heart beat steadily. If only she was nine again, not nineteen, almost twenty. She'd do things so differently.

"Why are you so good to me?" Molly winced. It came out more whine than question.

"I'm not sure." Blue stopped, and she closed her eyes. *Here it comes.* "I stepped in more out of instinct, but then you asked me to come with you, I couldn't say no. It just sort of snowballed from there. I've been deliberately a loner for years. But you brought out a part of me I thought I'd killed for good."

"Sorry." Molly fought back another sobbing fit.

"Sorry?" Blue brushed the top of her head. "I should be thanking you for helping feel human again."

"Really?" Her bruised heart wanted to believe him, but a cynical voice in her head said he was playing her. "What do you want out of this?"

"I haven't thought about it." Blue rocked her a bit. "I guess first, for you to be safe and happy. Then maybe, not to forget what I learned."

"I can't count how many people told me they wanted the best for me." Molly's mouth twisted at the bitter taste of her words.

"I bet they then told you what that was." Blue chuckled.

"Always, it somehow made their lives better, but not mine."

"What do you want to do?" He ran his hand down her back.

"Damned if I know." Molly shivered and cuddled closer.

"When you figure it out, I will help you."

"Why?"

"Helping you helps me."

Molly shook, and pain shot through her. Darkness pulled at her. She should go looking for a fix. The buzz would push the shadows back, dull the pain, blur the memories.

"I need a fix." She hadn't meant to say it out loud.

"I need a drink." Blue responded. "Every damn day I need a drink, for two years, I've needed that drink. Almost had one the other day, I could taste the beer, almost feel the alcohol hitting..." He ran down and took a deep breath. "I'm not helping much."

"You understand." Molly whispered. She pushed back the need. It wasn't the first time she'd had the shakes. "I need to go for a walk."

"That isn't a good idea." Blue relaxed his arms and let her go.

"But you're going to let me go." She stood up and hugged herself against the twitching in her muscles.

"Your choice." Blue stood. "I'll keep an eye on you." He grimaced and put a hand on his back.

"What did they do to you?"

"Stabbed me in the back. The jacket turned the blade, so it's more irritating than dangerous."

"Right." Molly headed along the path and picked up a stick which she swung about occasionally banging it on a tree. At the Halston bridge she had to climb up on the trail. Women jogged with three wheeled strollers. An old man went by on a scooter, a tiny dog on a leash leading him.

There were people at their camp last night. Would they still be there? But the need to move was as powerful as the desire for a fix. She wanted to break into a run, sprint until she collapsed with a burst heart. Instead, she settled for the fastest walk she could manage.

The path was crowded, and she had her stick.

No one rushed from the park to attack her. Her new boots made walking more comfortable. The path emptied past the park.

"Hey, Molly, what's up?" A guy leaned against a garden wall. "Haven't seen you on your patch."

"You know what it's like. Had to take off for a bit."

"Your Man isn't going to like that."

"Doesn't like anything I do." Molly hugged herself tighter.

"You look like you're needing a little fix." The guy leered at her. "A blow for a blow."

It would be so easy. She'd done it countless times, a few minutes, she'd get that rush, and everything would be better. *Every damn day I need a drink.* Blue's voice sounded in her head, as emotional as she'd ever heard him. He'd understand.

"No." Molly stepped back. "I'm hitching out of town. No one will pick me up if I'm high."

"They won't pick you up if you're jonesing for a fix either." He walked toward her, his face saying he wasn't going to take no for an answer.

She hoisted the stick.

"You think that little thing will stop me?" He lunged at her. Molly stabbed at him with the end. The guy grabbed it easily and pulled it away. While his hands were on the stick, she kicked his knee. The need to strike out, the fear, the anger, became a black rage.

Holding the cuff still dangling from her wrist under the over-long shirt sleeve, she slammed it into his face, then kicked the other knee. When he went down, she kept attacking him, stomping on his wrist when he tried to grab her leg.

An arm pulled her back, and she flailed wildly until suddenly she had no strength left to move.

"We should get out of here." Blue put her down on her feet, then caught her when she almost fell.

The guy lay still on the side of the trail.

"I did that?" Nausea struck her, and she puked up the little food in her stomach.

"Would you feel better if I told you he deserved it?"

"No." Molly forced her legs to hold her, then walked south. She threw the stick into the river, wanted to follow it; let the water drown her, wash everything away.

She made it almost back to Sam's tent before she fell. Blue picked her up without comment and carried her the rest of the way.

"Let's get that cuff off you. It will raise eyebrows" Blue used a bit of wire and a lot of fiddling to get them open. Then Molly crawled into the tent and collapsed on Sam's sleeping bag.

***

The smell of food dragged her out of her dream. She was kicking Tad, but he laughed at her, grabbing her throat and lifting her off the ground while her feet jerked and she gasped for air.

Molly stared at the dappled roof of the tent and tried to slow her heart. The stuffy tent didn't help, so she went outside. Sam handed her a bowl of chilli from a can. The warmth of the food eased her stomach.

"I want to stop Tad." Molly paused between mouthfuls.

"This isn't a movie." Blue frowned. "We can't go in with guns blazing, even if we had the guns. There are laws for reason and cops to enforce them."

"They haven't stopped him yet." Molly snapped back at him. "What do they need to do something?"

"Evidence." Blue's voice was flat, emotionless. "Enough to justify a warrant. Unless Tad is dumb to enough commit a crime in sight of a police officer."

"So he gets away with it."

"I'm sure officers are working on getting enough evidence to search his premises. But they won't if ask for a warrant if there's a chance they won't find anything."

"Useless." She glared at him as Sam refilled her bowl.

"It feels that way at times." Blue's eyes were looking past her at something only he could see. "We are playing chess against an opponent who cheats with impunity, but we have to follow the rules."

"We're not cops."

"No, we're not." Blue had gone from emotionless to cold. He stood up and walked away, leaving Molly with her mouth hanging open, spoon stopped halfway to her mouth.

"What do I do now?" She put her bowl down, appetite gone.

"You can't fight someone else's demons." Sam kept eating.

Molly tried to see through the gloom, but Blue had vanished.

CHAPTER 17
Saturday, May 11

Blue didn't pay any attention to where he walked. He'd shut down to keep from falling apart.

What was he doing? Molly wanted him to save her, and he couldn't even save himself. For years he'd run from himself, his failure. She didn't know how fragile the balance he'd created was.

You never told her.

The family at McDonald's, happy, excited, nothing out of the ordinary. The father in his suit and power tie hadn't even glanced in the direction of the cop in full uniform. When the call came over the radio, Blue had been closest, so he responded, following all the rules. Keep the man talking, bring in the experts. Keeping the person talking kept them from other things; it brought the risk down.

When the gun shot interrupted them, Blue decided he need to enter the home. The situation had changed, he'd reported to dispatch. He approached cautiously. Everything by the book.

The front door was unlocked. He pushed it open, and the smell hit him. Life as he knew it ended in that moment.

Blue put his hands to his face. Why was he thinking about this? He'd be no good to anyone curled up and broken.

But his mind took him through that door, into a room painted red with blood and things he didn't want to identify as what was left of children. A man leaned against the wall under the window, most of his head gone. The suit jacket was gone, but the power tie hung from his neck.

What could turn that happy family into this? He'd never found an answer. Could he have prevented it? What in the endless regulations allowed him to stop this tragedy?

The connection between Blue and his self shattered. He watched in his memories as he started drinking, first after his shift ended, then before. Suspensions piled up. The union suggested he apply for disability, but what was he if not a cop?

In the end, the decision was taken away from him. Indefinite medical leave, they called it. He walked out of the house he shared with his mother and never looked back.

Even when he'd sobered up, he never went back, never called her. What was he? Not a cop.

The moon hung over the river, cold and aloof. It would be a peaceful place to live, away from everything, no worries. Only that wasn't living. Living meant riding the currents, the ripples disturbing the image of perfection.

Molly dragged him back into the world. His life like a limb that had gone to sleep. It looked normal, but was numb, useless. Yet the pain of waking might kill him.

So be it.

His body moved before he was aware of the attack. The first punk stumbled past. He pushed the second one into the path of the fourth. The third he slapped the knife aside, gripped his shirt, then swept his forward leg out and slammed him on the ground. The punk bounced, then lay gasping and choking.

The first attacked again, kicking at Blue's head. He pulled the foot forward, stretching the kick until the kid was off balance, then hammered a blow into his thigh. An elbow to the head as the kid dropped would keep him down.

The second attacker came in slowly, his stance looking like he'd learned it from a martial arts movie. The fourth stood back, staring uncertainly, a knife held in a shaking hand.

The second guy rushed in, flailing blows. Blue sidestepped, then clotheslined him. The nervous one charged in and slashed while Blue was still hampered by the second. Blue took the blow on his left forearm, trusting to the heavy jacket to weaken the blow. He punched the guy in the solar plexus, folding the attacker around his fist, then drove his knee into the kid's face.

"You've pissed me off." Blue told them as he gathered up their knives, slapping away attempts to grab him. "Next time I won't be so gentle."

He threw the knives one after the other into the river, where the water stayed deep enough to never reveal them. His arm stung a bit where the knife had bit through the leather.

The walk back to camp allowed him to come down from the adrenaline high. Part of him reveled in the violence. He called it the beast, and it was as addictive as booze. None of them had sustained any major damage, but they'd be sore for a while.

Would they run to Tad and report? In their shoes, Blue wouldn't want to advertise their failure, but he couldn't count on that. Depending on your enemy's mistakes was a good way to get killed.

Sam waited for him by the tent. Molly probably slept in the tent.

"So?"

"Four punks jumped me." Blue rubbed his arm. "They are regretting it."

"You feel better?"

"Fighting can be worse than booze."

"That doesn't answer the question." Sam tore open a package of chocolate chip cookies and passed some over to Blue.

"Yes, I feel better. I've been avoiding dealing with stuff; Molly shook that up." He stuffed a cookie in his mouth.

"Kids will do that."

"You have any?"

"Two, one in Toronto, one in Japan." Sam took out another stack of cookies and waved the package in Blue's direction. "One grandkid in Toronto, one on the way in Japan." He waved at the tent and the burned down fire. "This is to save enough to fly over visit. I won't get there on my crappy pension."

"Sounds like a plan." Studied the older man. "You don't seem to be surprised by anything."

"Thirty years in the church will do that to you. I've broken up fights at funerals, talked grooms into not leaving their brides at the altar. Board meetings will scar you for life. I had a drinking problem, then an anger problem. Punched the choir director at a board meeting. He deserved it, but that's beside the point. After that, no one wanted me. I'm waiting until I'm sixty-five and will get enough to almost live on."

"I wouldn't have pegged you as an ex-pastor."

"You, on the other hand, exude ex-cop these days."

"Old habits." Blue munched on more cookies. "I'm thinking it is time to let it go. I'm no good if all I do is not be a cop."

"You've made a big step." Sam saluted him with chocolate stained hand. "Don't stop, there's still the next one."

"What's that?"

"The hell if I know." Sam rolled his eyes. "But there always is one."

"Helpful." Blue looked over at the tent. "I have business to clear up."

"Thought you were done with the cop thing."

"I am, but Molly won't be free until that punk is in jail."

"You have a plan?"

"Working on it."

Sam shifted in his seat. "She cried herself to sleep. Probably blaming herself for driving you away."

"We'll talk in the morning." Blue stretched. He should have retrieved his gear on his walk. It would be stupid to go now.

"You want an old man's advice? Talk to her now." Sam wrapped himself up in a tattered fleece blanket and closed his eyes.

Blue crept into the tent. Molly lay curled up, looking like a little kid in the oversized sweatshirt. His chest ached.

"Molly."

She came awake in an instant, eyes wide in panic. Then bolted upright to wrap her arms around Blue.

"Sorry." Blue put his cheek against her hair.

"I didn't think you were coming back." Molly's tears soaked through his shirt.

"I will always come back." Blue stepped over an invisible line he didn't know he'd drawn. "As long as I'm alive."

"You don't have to." Molly whispered.

"No, I don't. But I want to."

"I'm a hooker, a druggie, I'll just be trouble."

"The trouble part is probably true, but it is of everyone. The rest," Blue sighed. "we can't let what we used to be stop us."

"What happened to you?" Molly asked. "I promise myself I wouldn't ask, but I keep hurting you."

"I'll tell you, but it's enough to give you nightmares."

"I already have nightmares." She sat back, cross-legged on the sleeping bag.

Blue told her the whole story, not trying to hide his tears or the shaking in his voice.

When he'd finished, she stared at him, mouth gaping, tears on her cheeks. Then she moved over to wrap her arms around him.

"It's all right. I'm here."

***

"What part of quiet did you have problems understanding?" The boss' voice grated on Hank's ears. He kept stacking bags against the wall. Smaller bags filled the counter on the other side. The Nolan and the bruisers set up the table.

"She blew you right off, didn't she? Got rid of the evidence slick as shit too."

"So you snatch her, leave a witness, then allow her to escape, again." She pointed at him. "Any more screw ups and I may decide I need one last test subject. Watch them if you have to, but no action unless I say so." Her voice changed as if she'd flipped a switch. "We need packers. People who will keep their mouths shut. Get on it."

Tad glared at her back as she walked around the wall to get in her car. Hank kept his head down with any luck Tad would pick on someone else.

"Zac, print some shit to hand out like it's a real job."

"What do you want on it?"

"Easy money, a few days' work. They want to work, they meet you at the gazebo and you can bring them here. Then no one leaves until the work's done."

"Got it."

"Kid." Tad came over to Hank. "Here are the boss' instructions. You'll make sure they're followed exactly. Any screwups will be on your head." He pointed to a list of things they needed. "You've got money, go buy the shit we need, get a dozen sets."

"Sure." Hank dropped the bag in his hand on the pile and it poofed out a cloud of powder. "Anything you say."

First the jerk only paid him half, now he wants Tad to spend it. Maybe he could lift what he needed.

CHAPTER 18
Monday, May 13

"I'm not sitting around all day while you go looking for stuff." Molly had her hands on her hips, and Blue's stomach sunk.

"It isn't safe, Tad and his gang will be looking for you."

"Let them." Molly glared at him. "When they grabbed me, it wasn't from the street, but from the camp. Who's to say they won't do that again?"

"She has a point." Sam looked up from where he was tidying up his tent.

"What do you have in mind?" Blue's resolve was slipping away from him.

"Talk to the other girls. The guys treated us like they're deaf and dumb, but we know a lot more than they think."

"Right, let's go over everything we know." Blue's fingers itched for a notebook.

"Nolan, Tad's second said something about the long weekend. That's this week." Molly relaxed into a thoughtful posture.

"Rooster told me the aliens had the best drugs." Blue scrubbed his fingers through his hair. "That was the night before he died. There was a needle beside him, though he was phobic about needles."

"Too many of the ODs have had needles still in them. Who leaves the thing in after they've injected?" Sam said. "Like someone is saying 'look it's an overdose'. The aliens are covering their tracks."

Blue sat back and stared into the blue sky. "Okay, first we need new clothes. Molly, that means not black. Make people work hard to spot us."

"Black just means I don't have to worry about what matches." She grinned. "I could get into a little colour."

"As far as anyone knows, I have nothing to do with you." Sam set up his chair and settled into it. "I'll wait here while you kids go shopping."

Blue rolled his eyes while Molly rubbed her hands together. They walked to Penny Pinchers where she picked out blue jeans, a pair of red pants and a handful of blouses in different colours, then a tiny black purse. Blue grabbed a hoodie and a few t-shirts to go under it. He topped it off with a bucket hat, sending Molly into a fit of giggles. She found a white baseball hat for herself.

"Stay on the street." Blue carried the bag of extra clothes. "Don't go with someone into alleys or buildings for any reason. If you need the washroom, use the one at Timmies." He handed her some change. "We'll meet up at McDonald's."

"What if I'm followed?" She put the change in her purse.

"Pay attention to the people around you. Most people who follow you won't fit into the flow. They'll stop at odd times, or too abruptly. Don't try to lose them. If you think you're in danger, watch for a police officer and tell them someone's following you. If you don't see one, go into a busy store and tell the clerk."

"Gotcha." Molly clenched and relaxed her hands, tugged the sleeve of the blouse down to hide the needle marks on her arm.

"Get the nerves out of your system now. If you act afraid, people will notice."

"What are you going to be doing?"

"I will scout out that side-by-side, see what I can learn about Tad's operation."

"Be careful, Nolan is meaner than Tad is, and there are two big guys who do whatever they're told. A few hangers on work for free sex and drugs."

"Got it."

They arrived back at the camp.

"Going to listen for aliens." Sam put his hands in his pockets and strolled away.

***

Blue followed Molly at a distance. He'd grabbed a shopping cart from the side of the road and picked through recycle dumpsters to find junk to fill it. Rolling the hoodie in the mud made it look old and dirty. More dirt on his face completed the picture. He hated playing to the cliché of the dirty street bum, but people wouldn't look past the grime. He hoped.

She sashayed south along Tranquille. If he hadn't known what she was wearing, he might have missed her himself.

Hank stood with a clump of other punks and didn't bat an eye when she went past. A woman leaning against a tree watched, but didn't move until Molly was well past.

Blue pushed his cart, keeping his head down and taking in the scene with quick glances.

Across from the Big Edition office, two young women lounged on the grassy hill. Molly joined them. The three laughed at something Molly said. The woman watching them kept going. Blue stayed with her.

Tad waited near the liquor store.

"She's chatting with a couple of girls. Not a care in the world." The woman spoke like the words tasted bitter, and he recognized Hannah.

"Didn't think she could resist looking for action. Never did have much tolerance for doing nothing." Tad ground a fist against his other hand. "Leave her be, let her start feeling safe and she'll get careless." He handed her something. "Go relax, it's on me."

Blue rooted about in the garbage a bit longer, then dodged a kick from Tad and kept going down the street. He turned a corner later than the woman, then trundled along the alley. The woman walked into the house Molly had described as Tad's headquarters. A stain above a boarded-up window might have been blood.

He kept going, stopping to poke around and pick up bottles or cans.

At least I'm cleaning up the streets. Blue headed back to camp until it was time to meet Molly.

***

Molly laughed with Tiff and Jice. They weren't working girls, but partiers she'd known while in the system. Rumours of a new drug filled them with speculation.

"Something called Black Death or something," Tiff said. "Supposed to be the closest thing to a near death experience you can get without dying." She kept babbling on about how she couldn't wait to try it. Jice said nothing and looked stoned.

"Heard there were aliens around abducting people." Molly faked a shudder.

"No, it's ghosts." Jice sounded like one herself. "The spirits of the dead wanting to party again." She giggled, and Molly didn't have to fake the shiver.

Heading back up to McDonald's, Molly kept an eye out for any of Tad's women. They were always tattling on the others, making up tales about the girls holding back money. Molly thought she'd spotted a woman tailing her, but the walk was uneventful. She slid into a booth with a pop and fries, Blue sat in his leather jacket with his back to her in the next booth.

After she'd had her snack, Molly left, heading back to their camp. Blue would be behind her and deal with anyone following.

***

Blue slipped out from under the sleeping bag and wrapped it tighter around Molly. He put on the hoodie and slipped out of camp. From the moon, it had to be after two in the morning. Almost everyone would be done for the night.

The streets were deserted except for a few deer who looked at him, then cantered away.

Blue prowled around the side-by-side, but couldn't see much from the outside. All the windows had drawn curtains, the lower windows were painted shut. Security cameras watched the doors, front and back.

The creak of a hinge made him flatten himself on the ground against the wall.

A big man closed the back door and walked with surprising grace to the alley. Blue didn't think he'd want to tangle with that one. He walked along the street in the same direction, then hunched in a bush's shadow to see where the man would go next.

The big man led him east to Tranquille, then to the Overland Bridge. Blue contented himself with watching him cross over before he headed back to the camp.

What was one of Tad's men doing crossing the bridge to the south shore? That was a different territory. Either he was reporting to another gang, or the Boss Molly mentioned didn't live on the North Shore.

Whatever, time to get back.

***

Molly elbowed him when he lay back down.

"You'd better have a good reason for leaving without telling me."

"Sorry, I didn't want to wake you."

"Did you at least learn anything?"

"I think Tad has a security problem." He explained what he'd seen.

"Tad isn't the smartest of people." Molly leaned on her elbow to look at Blue. "If he was working for me, I'd want someone keeping an eye on him."

***

Hank finished showing the girl how to cut and measure the drug. This was the third time, he expected she'd forget again. Didn't look like she had much of a brain left. Her friend was a little better.

"Keep an eye on her. She screws up, you both get docked." Hank put his tough guy voice on, but neither girl looked impressed. *Why do I keep getting these shit jobs?*

He moved on to a man and woman working with laser-like focus. They'd done a line of something before they started. Probably meth from the looks of it. Tad wouldn't care as long as the tiny baggies got filled with something approximating the mix that witch of a boss demanded.

How many of these people will get paid, and how many would just vanish?

Hank didn't want to be one of the ones who vanished.

"No, no." He ran back to the stoner girl. "Do it right, or we're all in trouble."

CHAPTER 19
Tuesday, May 14

"We didn't learn much yesterday." Molly sat, chin on her knees, staring into Sam's tiny fire.

"No new stories about aliens or ghosts." Sam shifted the pot on the grate to centre it over the heat better. "But some are worried about the plague."

"Plague?" Blue lifted his head.

"The Black Death." Molly put a tiny stick into the fire. "If you didn't know it was a drug, wouldn't it make you nervous?"

"Have to wonder why they named it that." Sam dug out a tea bag.

"Tiff said something about it being a near death experience." Molly frowned. "Maybe it's like playing Russian roulette. The danger is part of the rush."

"Wouldn't surprise me." Blue stretched, then pulled out the peanut butter and bread. Molly took them and started making sandwiches. "If the only thing to look forward to is poverty and boredom, risking death for a thrill isn't much of a stretch."

"They're probably hoping for more of the rich and bored market." Sam poured the tea and handed Blue a cup.

"What do we do today?" Molly waved away the tea and munched on a sandwich.

"More listening." Blue blew on his tea. "See who comes out of the woodwork."

She rolled her eyes.

"Detective work is boring as hell." Blue tried a sip and burned his tongue. "At least if you're doing it right. Nothing like the movies."

"So no rocket launchers then?" Molly grinned at him.

"No rocket launchers." Blue grinned back. "All we want is enough for a decent tip to the cops. I'd like to know where they have the drugs. I doubt the stuff is at the house you escaped from. Too many people around to keep it secret."

"That's the only place I know of." Molly shrugged and took another huge bite.

"Maybe it's a place this Boss set up, not Tad." Blue set his tea down and plastered another slice of bread with peanut butter. "Which reminds me." He told them about the man sneaking out of the house.

"Is that something we can use?" Molly leaned forward, eyes bright.

"Maybe, at the right time. If we get them fighting, then there's a chance they'll make a mistake."

***

Molly walked south on Tranquille watching the people. On a Tuesday afternoon, the crowds weren't that heavy. Nobody looked to be paying her any attention. She didn't see Tiff or Jice, but someone lounged against a tree wearing a familiar pink jacket.

"You're new." Molly leaned against the tree so she could just see the other woman in the corner of her eye.

"This is my pitch." The woman glared at her.

"I'm not in the business."

"Not what I heard." The woman stroked the leather jacket. "Still living on your back with that old guy. What will you do when he gets bored with you?"

"Worry about it when it happens."

"Tad will take you back."

"Like hell he will." Molly laughed. "Last I heard he was selling me to the coast. Besides, he's got bigger problems than me."

"Did you enjoy the little gift I gave you?" The woman sneered. "He's got connections everywhere."

"He also has delusions of grandeur." Molly snorted. "I spotted your plant first thing and dumped it. Pretty lame."

"You want your jacket back; you'll have to fight me for it."

"Nah, it suits you, makes you look like a granny pretending to be young." Molly skipped away from the other woman's clawed hands. "Careful, you could break a nail that way."

"I'm going to beat you bloody." The woman lunged at Molly. The whoop of a siren startled her. She turned and ran off as the police car parked and a cop climbed out.

"You all right?" The constable was the one who'd stopped her when she was selling papers.

"Sure," Molly put on her best smile, "she's just a little high."

The cop looked up, but the pink jacket was nowhere to be seen on the street.

"You be careful, miss. Not everyone is safe to talk to."

"Thank you, officer."

He returned to the cruiser and drove away. Molly giggled, being polite to the police felt weird.

She wandered along the street to the Big Edition office and thought about going in. No matter what she'd said to that old hooker, losing the jacket hurt. Maybe she could earn enough to buy another one.

Next month, there aren't enough people to buy the paper around, anyway.

On her walk north, a young man hailed her. He looked vaguely familiar, maybe one of Tad's groupies.

"Hey cutie."

He sat on the curb in front of Timmies.

"What do you want?" Molly eyed him suspiciously.

"You want a job? Easy money, just a few day's work."

"I've heard that one before. No thanks."

"Whatever." He shrugged and turned away from her.

As she walked on, Molly debated what the kid was up to. Something more than just easy money, but he also didn't look like the usual recruiter for girls. She stopped to look in a window and saw him talking to middle-aged street people pushing a cart. Definitely not recruiting girls. He handed them a card which the man peered at suspiciously, then put in his pocket.

The kid stood up and dusted off his pants, then walked away behind Timmies. Molly almost followed him, but Blue would blow a gasket. She turned and continued north.

***

"You were smart to leave it alone." Blue had a worried look, furrows lining his forehead. "All it would take would be one person to spot you and you'd be in deep trouble. That kind of thing takes a lot of preparation, and even then, it's dicey."

"Figured." Molly dug into the peanut butter. They were getting low.

"You know anyone named Brad?" Sam looked up from where Molly thought he'd been sleeping in his chair.

Blue went still, and Molly worried he would pass out his face was so pale.

"Why do you want to know?" Molly asked. Blue didn't look ready to say anything.

"I got a text saying my voicemail was full and would I check it." Sam pulled out his phone and peered at it. "No one but my kids have this number, and they'd text me, not phone. I keep it turned off most of the time."

"And?" Blue's hands were shaking. Molly put down the bread and took his hand.

"Some woman wanting to talk to Brad; could I get a message to him? Five, six calls a day." Sam handed the phone to Blue. "Then I thought to look at what number you'd called, since they started the day after you'd borrowed my phone. Recognize it?"

Molly looked at the phone in Blue's hand. The number he'd called belonged to an agency named 'unHooked'.

"I can't." Blue pushed the phone into Molly's hands. "She'd hate me for what I've become."

"This doesn't look like hate." Molly scrolled through the endless list of missed calls.

"You tell her I'm okay." Blue stumbled out of the camp.

Now Molly's hands shook. Her finger tapped the phone before she thought of what to say.

"Hello?" The voice on the other end sounded tired, desperate.

"Hi, my name is Molly."

"Right," the woman became cool, professional, "let me get a pen and paper, Molly. Now, what can I do for you?"

"You help girls get off the street, right?"

"That's right. We have a one-year residential program, then we follow up periodically after that with counselling."

"A friend suggested I call." Molly's mouth went dry and her heart pounded. "He said his mother ran it."

The silence went on so long Molly was afraid the call had dropped. She wiped her palms on her pants. Sam looked on imperturbably.

"You know Brad?"

"He doesn't call himself that," Molly said. "Everyone knows him as Blue."

"Is he well?"

"He's saved my life more than once, but he's afraid." She wiped the tears from her eyes. "He's afraid you'll hate him."

"Never." The woman sounded like she was fighting her own tears. "But this thing…" Sobbing came from the phone.

"He told me." Molly wanted to reach in and hug this woman. "Blue wanted me to know I wasn't the only broken one."

"That sounds like Brad." The woman took a deep breath. "Can I contact you at this number?"

"Send a text." Molly looked over at Sam, who gave a thumbs up.

"I will do that, then I can do a proper intake, I'm just... tell Brad his mom loves him." The woman disconnected the call.

Molly handed the phone back to Sam, then collapsed on the sleeping bag and wailed.

CHAPTER 20

Blue's chest tightened until he could barely breathe. His heart raced, and the lights across the river blurred.

This panic attack didn't bring up visions of the red room, or the family at McDonald's. Instead, it showed him his mother growing more worried as he slipped into the booze, trying to keep the demons at bay. It never worked, only destroyed what little he had left.

That last day he'd walked out in a drunken rage, never to return, or even call. They'd put him on indefinite sick leave, took away what made him, him. Couldn't yell at the bureaucrats, so he yelled at his mother, cutting the last connection with who he was.

The real miracle was that she'd recognized his voice from those few stumbling words. No wonder she'd called, left so many messages.

He'd never expected to hear that name again. He'd cut all ties with his past. At least he'd thought they had been.

The water ran past; he concentrated on watching it, the currents and eddies revealed by the lights of the city. Gradually the ache decreased, and he could breathe, the damp air of the night washed through his lungs.

Going back to living like no one cared about him wasn't possible. But did he know how to not be alone? What if he hurt his mother again?

You already are, every day.

"Blue." A young man stepped out of the shadows.

"Hank." Blue tensed, waiting for an attack.

"I'm alone." Hank held his hands out to his side. "I just want to talk."

"I'm listening."

"Blue, I want out, and you're going to help me."

"Why?"

"I could threaten you, offer to tell Tad where you are, but I'm not going to." Hank twisted his hands together. "Why d'you make me look good in front of the gang?"

"It was easier." Blue responded automatically, but then thought about it. "You went after me because Tad humiliated you, and you couldn't take him. Who would have been next if I'd done the same thing?"

The kid stared at Blue.

"Somebody has to be the adult, to break the chain." Blue shrugged and more tension vanished. "If it isn't me, who will?"

"That's it?" Hank sounded disappointed.

"Listen, Hank. Don't let life be what other people think of you. If you do, you'll be miserable. I will not rescue you from the gang. You'll do that yourself, but I'll be there to help if I can."

"But..."

Faint wailing came through the night, making Blue's heart skip a beat.

"What's that?" Hank paled and backed away.

"Meet me at McDonald's tomorrow at noon." Blue ran back toward the camp.

Molly lay on the sleeping bag. Sam watched over her.

"She needs you," he said. "I'm going to hit the sack."

Blue dropped beside Molly and scooped her up to rock her until her wails quieted and she hiccupped.

"I want my mom to call and say she loves me." Molly spoke into Blue's chest. "Only she left me behind like an old shirt. I'll never even know her name."

"Molly." Blue hugged her tight.

"Do you love me? If I went away, would you worry about me? Would you call and call and call?" She started weeping again.

"I..." Blue hung on a precipice. "Molly, my life will never be the same because I met you. I would worry if you went away. If I had your phone number, I'd call."

"Really?" She sniffled and looked up at him.

"I'll introduce you to my mom, and you can share her."

"I'd like that." Molly snuggled against him and fell asleep. He put her down and wrapped the bag around her.

Do I love her? He brushed hair back from her face. *I'm not even sure what that means. I'd die to protect her. Maybe that's enough.*

***

At the garage Hank watched bleary eyed as the packers did their job, if not perfectly, at least not completely screwed up. They got more sleep than he did. Only the memory of Dan kept him from doing a line to stay awake.

Tad stopped in to sneer and find fault, but Hank was too exhausted to care. He leaned against the wall to keep from falling over.

The garage door clanked and rumbled open, then shut, and the boss woman came around the wall a few minutes later in tyvex and face mask. The people at the table wore cheap cloth things. At least Hank still had his industrial quality one with a filter. No way he wanted to breathe in that dust.

"How are we doing?"

Hank pointed to the boxes. She picked out two packets and inspected them before tossing them back in.

"Too slow. Get a couple more people."

"Hank can pack." Tad lounged in the chair.

"Hank is supervising." The woman pointed at him. "He's just about asleep on his feet. You watch the packers while he rests."

"I have things to do." Tad's face darkened, and he stomped out of the garage.

"Idiot." The woman pulled out her phone and sent a text. "Nolan will be here soon."

Tad took a deep breath.

"Can I talk to you for a minute?" Hank approached the boss.

"What do you want?" The woman's voice, even muffled, cut him cold.

"I have a deal I want to make with you..."

She jerked her thumb toward the chairs. "I think we can make that work. Get some sleep. I'll stay until Nolan gets here."

***

At McDonald's Blue waited in the corner for Hank to show up. At one p.m. he gave up and returned to camp.

"Okay, thanks." Molly was talking into Sam's phone when he got back to camp. It was plugged into something that looked like a brick with a red light flashing on it. "Let me know." She looked up when Blue arrived and held the phone out to him. He sat down abruptly and stared at the thing.

"Molly? You still there?" The question came from the phone.

"Mom," Blue couldn't get his voice above a whisper. Molly sat at his back, holding his free hand. "It's Brad."

"Molly said you're going by Blue now."

"Yeah, I didn't like Brad much."

"You taking care of yourself?" Blue could imagine her at her desk, playing with a pen, ready to take notes in an instant.

"Been sober two years." Blue closed his eyes and tried to imagine her face.

"That's wonderful. Sounds like you've helped Molly a lot."

"It just sort of happened, Mom. I have no idea what I'm doing." Molly squeezed his hand. "I could really use your help."

"You can always call."

"I know, I should have called sooner. I'm sorry."

"You're talking to me now, that's what matters."

The battery indicator on the phone flashed red.

"Phone's dying. I'll call you again."

"Love you, Blue." The phone went dead and Blue carefully set it to the side, then put his head on his knees.

"You okay?" Molly turned and wrapped her arms around him.

"Thank you." Blue closed his eyes and let the tears run down his cheeks. "I couldn't have done it without you."

138

"What now?" Molly put her head on his shoulder.

"I'm not sure." Blue's stomach tensed. "Hank didn't show. It could be him changing his mind again, or something else."

"Tad likes to keep everyone on a short leash." Molly stood up to pace. "It's why he's so determined to get me back, to show that no one escapes."

"Maybe he needs a distraction." Blue pushed himself up. "I'll watch the house again tonight and make contact."

"Be careful." Molly's pacing speeded up. "Those guys are bad news."

"I'll keep my distance." Blue tried to smile reassuringly, but from Molly's face, he didn't succeed terribly well. "While I go check out the territory, stay close to camp."

"I will."

Blue changed into the hoodie and dirtied his face. His pants didn't need much to look filthy. He walked toward Tranquille. There weren't any handy abandoned carts, so he picked up a plastic bag and filled it with whatever he found.

A man he didn't recognize lounged on the steps to the house. The reek of weed made it as far at Blue as he shambled along the street. He didn't see any other activity. He walked to MacDonald Park and did a circuit, looking closer at the whole neighbourhood. Everything looked peaceful, lawns cut, the occasional bike or toy in the yard. A few of the houses had big sheds in the backyard with garage doors.

Time to get back to camp. He'd need to be rested for when it got dark.

***

Molly couldn't sit still. She worried about Blue going up against any of Tad's thugs. He still had stitches from the attack on their camp. Sam's phone was dead, so he'd gone to the Mall to charge it and buy more food.

She stood on the riverbank and shivered, though she wore Blue's black leather jacket. Rubbing her fingers along the sleeve, she sighed. That pink jacket had been awesome, and Blue bought it for her. The first time she'd voluntarily worn anything but black since before she'd aged out. Black was easy, cheap. It sent the message not to screw with her. Then Tad had her wearing it because some clients liked tough girls.

Was I ever tough? She remembered trying to be tough, swearing, fighting, but couldn't recall ever feeling she'd made it. Looking back, it was hard to even think what she'd been trying so hard to accomplish. Sure, foster care had been hell, but a good portion of that was her own fault. Rebelling against rules, challenging the system, just for the sake of 'not giving in.'

What would have happened if she'd been more like she was with Blue; give and take, mutual respect? Too late now, couldn't turn the clock back, but she could change how she went forward.

Blue asked what she wanted, and she'd answered with a short-term goal of ridding Kamloops of Tad and his ilk. What did she want? Living without a home was okay for now; she had Blue and Sam to help, but eventually she'd need to live without depending on them.

She didn't even have a high school diploma, skipping more classes than she attended and ignoring every plea to work a bit harder for her own sake. No wonder she didn't see any other alternative to hooking to stay alive. What kind of job could she do?

There were lots of part-time minimum wage jobs which wouldn't pay the bills. Working that hard to be poor didn't appeal to her.

I don't even know what I need to learn.

She picked up a stick and tossed it into the river and watched the current carry it away.

Something poked her in the back.

"Behave yourself and you won't get hurt." At least it wasn't Tad. She darted away, but only got a few steps before a shove between her shoulder blades sent her face first into the ground. The person grabbed the collar of the jacket and hoisted her to her feet, then clenched a fistful of hair.

"Walk." Hank pushed her forward without slacking his hold on her. A woman in a suit tapped her foot on the walking path.

"Either kill her or let her walk on her own so it isn't obvious we're abducting her."

Molly recognized the voice.

"You're the lawyer who gave the cop a hard time."

"I'm no lawyer, you know how long it takes to be a lawyer? I work in her office as a clerk and dress the part." The woman looked insulted. "I'm a businesswoman."

"This is business?" Molly glared over her shoulder at Hank holding a knife at the ready.

"Think of it as a job interview."

"Right."

"Convince me you're worth something, or Hank slices your throat and puts you in the river."

"Go ahead, I'm not hooking anymore."

"We need packers, Boss. She looks smart enough not to wreck every second bag."

"Very well." They reached the parking lot where Hank shoved her into the back seat of a car, then slid in beside her.

"Buckle up." He wiggled the knife at his side.

"You will not get blood in my car." The boss climbed in and started the engine. "It's impossible to get out of the upholstery, and I just had it detailed."

They drove through back streets to a cinderblock building with a tall garage door. It opened as they approached, and she drove inside.

"Out."

Hank dragged her out of the car. A cinderblock wall with a gap on either end divided the building in half. An old RV parked over a pit in the floor. The boss drove away as soon as Hank closed the car door.

"At least she isn't high." Nolan closed the garage door.

Hank pushed Molly past the partial wall to where six people stood at a table working with piles of white powder. *Shit.* He handed her a mask and latex gloves.

"Wear this. Take it off and you get smacked. Do it twice and..." He held up the knife, Nolan rolled his eyes, but didn't say anything. "This is what you need to do." Hank picked up two measuring spoons. "The larger one is for the cornstarch, the smaller one the product, measure, even it off with this stick, then put it in this bowl. Mix the stuff, don't get it all over the place. Put it in one of these bags."

142

Bags of drugs were stacked like bricks against one wall, larger bags of cornstarch against the wall behind her. The others around the table worked like robots, though one girl muttered the instructions to herself constantly. Jice, Tiff worked beside her. Neither girl looked healthy. The others were people in old clothes, probably off the street. *That kid offering easy work.*

Molly started working. The longer she stayed alive, the longer Blue had to rescue her, though she didn't know how he could. This wasn't anywhere close to the cathouse. Even the windows were blacked out to keep the light from shining. From the outside, it was impossible to see anything.

Measure, stir, fill. Molly slipped into the rhythm, feeling like a robot herself. One man walked over to a corner and pulled out a cigarette.

"Idiot." Nolan stormed over and snatched the cigarette away and took the lighter. "You want to blow the place up?"

Molly didn't see how a cigarette could cause an explosion, but the guy actually looked scared, so she figured it had to be a risk.

Every couple of hours one of them got a break to drink some water and use the really disgusting washroom. They even had sandwiches to eat. The garage was hot and stuffy, so she took off Blue's jacket and tossed it in the corner.

The work was boring. The gloves and the mask were irritating as hell. Molly's back ached from constantly leaning forward. The pile of tiny bags grew. Then Hank would pack them into a box. The number of boxes grew slowly. Without a clock, time meant nothing. At one point, Molly,

Jice and Tiff were locked into the RV to sleep, then put back to work.

With each bag she packed, Molly's hope for rescue lessened.

***

Hank watched the packers work. He considered doing some himself, but Tad made it clear he was to watch and make sure they did at least a half-assed job of it. Nolan leaned against the wall, looking like he was part of it. Twice he took out his phone to look at it, but didn't respond to anything.

The boredom was torture. Hank walked around the table peering at the packers, but that didn't help. The smoker eyed the lighter Nolan had dropped on the desk in the corner, so Hank put it in his pocket. He didn't want to take any chances with something that made Nolan nervous.

The boss had promised him a way out if he brought in Molly and finished this packing job properly. She didn't expect them to do the whole thing yet wanted enough to flood the city over the weekend.

The image of the corpses they'd dumped, sticking needles in their arms, flashed through his mind. He didn't have a choice, did he? Tad would have killed him or had one of the bruisers do it. This was the only way out, and he'd take it no matter the cost. If Blue had offered some help... but he'd told Hank to work it out himself. This was how it went.

The night dragged on; he let the workers grab a nap, then kept them at it. The dealers would be getting the stuff Thursday night. His freedom depended on it.

None of that stopped him from feeling like shit every time Molly looked at him with ever increasing despair in her eyes.

CHAPTER 21

Blue walked into the empty camp, and his heart almost stopped. He checked by the river, but found neither Molly nor Sam.

Just as he was ready to run to the police station and try to get hold of Constable Madoc, Sam returned.

"What's up?"

"Molly's gone."

"Damn." Sam carried the bag of food to his tent. "What do we do?"

"You stay here in case she just got bored and wandered off." Blue looked around. "You see my leather jacket?"

"Nope, it's chilly. Molly must be wearing it."

Blue paced about the camp. He needed a plan. Running about aimlessly wouldn't help her. First would be staking out the house she'd escaped from. If he found something resembling an excuse for an emergency call... but it had to get the police through the door with reason to search the place. Easier said than done.

"I'm going to start with that house." Blue said. "Don't be surprised if I don't show up for a while. I have to wait for the opportunity to make a move."

"I'm not going anywhere." Sam frowned. "I shouldn't have left her alone. Don't know how they found us."

"I do." Blue clenched his fists. "And he will regret being born by the time I'm done with him."

"Don't do anything you won't be able to live with." Sam settled into his chair.

"Right."

Blue loped away, not worrying about the odd looks the occasional dog walker gave him. When he got to the house, it was still too light to do much more than walk past and look for a place to hole up. There wasn't much. Anywhere he stayed in place, someone would spot him, either from Tad's gang or the neighbours. It also needed to let him monitor access to both front and back doors.

He walked around the block a couple of times before worrying someone would wonder about him. Even as the light dimmed, he didn't think he could safely hide in the hedge across the street, and it only let him watch the front door. In the back alley, there were more nooks, but security lights became a problem.

Molly had waited them out on the roof, but a branch which bent under her weight could break with his.

That didn't stop him from using the tree. It wasn't ideal, with a line of sight on the back door, but not the front. The bruiser had used the back, so maybe that was okay. A plan formed in his mind. Risky, as a cop, he would never have even considered it.

Blue scrambled up into the tree and made himself as comfortable as he could. If he was going to follow the bruiser, he had a long wait ahead of him.

He didn't believe any of the movies or books that talked about sleeping in a tree. Even if he'd been tired enough to sleep, the discomfort would have made it impossible. The bark jabbed into his back; the limbs were at the wrong angle. The hand he steadied himself with cramped, then went numb. The leather jacket would have offered more protection, but he'd have to do without.

The moon rose and played peekaboo through the clouds. Cars drove past, and a few people passed walking dogs, or as couples holding hands.

The night passed slowly, and the traffic slowed, then stopped. The lights in the windows went out around him, one by one until only a few porch lights added to the streetlight two houses down. The alley filled with stygian darkness, once in a while lightened by a gleam from the moon through a gap in the cloud cover.

The back door creaked open. No light came on. The crunch of shoes on gravel indicated where he walked.

Blue waited until he couldn't hear the sound before dropping out of the tree, biting back a groan at the agony of moving again. He hobbled after his target. At least he knew where the guy was going, and the stiffness would work out as he walked.

The bruiser lit a cigarette, making it easy to keep an eye on him, but Blue needed to catch up at a place where he could talk to the man without putting himself at risk. He wanted to do it before the long open span of the bridge would give him away.

"Keep walking." The voice behind him sounded more bored than threatening. The red glow of the cigarette bobbed along ahead of him. "You aren't very good at this."

Blue swore under his breath but had no choice but to do what he was told for the moment.

"How long have you been selling Tad out?"

"You think that gives you a hold over me?" The man behind him snorted. "Dream on."

"I'm looking for a girl." Blue kept his voice casual. "The one who did a runner on Tad. She owes me money."

"Don't care about that." The voice sounded bored. "I only discipline them when I'm told. But the moron was angry enough to do his own work on that one. That worked out *so* well for him."

The one with the cigarette leaned against a post.

"Just three friends walking home late." The click of a knife opening accompanied the words.

Blue prayed for a car to come along. Maybe he could get across the bridge, but a shadow leaned on the railing there too.

"I had this feeling someone tailed me the other night, so I made some arrangements." The man with the knife sounded bored.

They reached the middle of the bridge and the moon found a gap in the clouds long enough to reveal the smirk on the bruiser's face. Blue kicked out at the knife as the other man wrapped an arm around his neck. The bruiser laughed and caught Blue's foot.

"So predictable." He hoisted Blue up and tossed his legs over the railing. "From this height, the water might as well be concrete."

The strangle hold released, and a hand shoved the middle of his back, then he was falling.

Years ago, he'd gone camping and jumped off a cliff. Feet crossed, toes pointed, hand protecting his face. Blue flailed, trying to right himself. No matter how many times he'd jumped from that cliff, the quickness of the fall always caught him off guard.

He slammed into the water, knocking the air out of his lungs. The icy cold made him want to scream, but he had nothing left to make a sound.

Underwater, nothing gave him a clue about up or down. As hard as he fought, he might have been diving deeper, not heading for the surface. A couple of weeks ago, he wouldn't have bothered. The end would have been welcome.

Molly.

Blue broke the surface and gasped for air, forcing himself to be silent, though his lung demanded he shriek. He fought his way toward the shore, dropping the hoodie into the depths of the river, but refusing to shed his boots. He needed them to track the S.O.B.s who'd taken the girl who'd given him purpose in live again.

When he crawled onto the shore, Blue had no strength left and lay gasping on the mud.

I didn't survive the river to die here.

He staggered to his feet. The camp wasn't far. Not when he was strong. Now he shook violently, but he kicked himself into motion. Get to camp, get warm, then rescue Molly. *Like it will be that easy.* The walk was a nightmare, no matter how he pushed himself it felt like he fought his way through jello.

Finally, as he despaired of finding safety, the light of the fire reached out.

"Sam." He meant to shout, but it came out as a gargled cry. Miraculously Sam stood up and ran to him, then half carrying him back to the camp. He stripped the wet clothes from Blue and made him sit wrapped in the sleeping bag while he built up the fire.

"What happened?" Sam put water on to heat, then dragged out Blue's gear bag to pull out the wool clothes.

"Got careless." Blue's teeth chattered. "Ended up in the river."

"I'm surprised they let you get away with a dunking."

"Off the bridge, they think I'm dead."

"And you're alive?" Sam's eyes widened. "Someone's looking out for you."

"Wish he'd started a lot earlier." The shivering lessened. Blue didn't know if that was a good thing.

"Life isn't about being easy." Sam put tea in the pot and got out the cups. "It's about doing what we can despite the shit show."

"Strange." Blue changed the subject; religion wasn't something he wanted to talk about. "The guy didn't know about Molly. He only knew about the first time when she escaped."

"Tad didn't grab her?" Sam poured the tea, adding several heaping spoons of sugar to Blue's cup.

"Maybe that boss Molly mentioned. Hank must've made a deal with her." He sipped the tea and made a face.

"Drink it, you need the boost." Sam pointed at him.

Blue drank the tea.

"I don't think she's at the house. That bruiser would have known about it. Even if he didn't answer, he would have reacted differently."

"Where else could they have her?"

"They're making a push toward putting that Black Death shit on the street this weekend." Blue put the cup down, Sam immediately refilled it and handed it back.

"Where are they keeping that stuff?"

"Could be anywhere. No, has to be close enough for Tad to keep an eye on things. Also needs to be someplace people can't see in the windows, and where a certain amount of coming and going is expected." Blue fought to keep his eyes open but was losing the battle.

"Get some sleep." Sam picked up the cup. "You're no good exhausted."

***

Molly worked mechanically, Jice still muttered under her breath, but she was pale and sweating. Molly worried about her to distract herself from worry for her herself.

Hank had left soon after they were put back to work, Nolan lounged in a corner watching them.

Molly waved at Nolan. "Hey, this girl's sick."

"So?" Nolan didn't move. "What d'ya want me to do about it?"

Jice's eyes rolled up in her head and she collapsed. Nolan swore and dragged her away from the table, then went to fetch the others resting in the RV.

"Is she going to be all right?" Molly whispered to Tiff.

"How the hell should I know?" Tiff glared at Molly as if it was all her fault.

The others took their places, and time passed at a glacial pace. Molly couldn't help but wonder where Blue was. Part of her knew she was being unreasonable. How could he know where she was? She didn't have more than the vaguest of notions.

"This isn't a movie." He'd said to her when he'd said they couldn't go in guns blazing. Blue had only spoken the truth. In real life there were no last-minute dramatic rescues, but for a few precious days she'd escaped the harsh life of the street. She'd even believed it would last.

Tears blurred her vision, and she wiped her eyes with the back of her arm.

"Don't be crying into the product." Nolan slapped the back of her head. "Unless you want to join her." He jerked his thumb in Jice's direction. The only sign she still lived was the wheezing of her breathing.

Molly wanted to beat him with something, knock him down and kick his head until it cracked open. The fierceness of her desire to kill him took her by surprise and stopped the tears. She laughed.

"What's so funny?"

"Sorry, I actually expected you to act like a human for a second. Should have remembered you're a cockroach with muscles."

Nolan grabbed her by the throat and put a gun against her forehead.

"Careful, don't want to get blood in the product." Molly giggled.

"I'll kill you." Nolan's hand squeezed tighter.

"Please." Molly held his gaze.

"Now, you're begging for your life?" Nolan leered at her.

"No, moron." Molly spat on him. "I want you kill me. Come on tough guy, pull the trigger. Strangle me, whatever."

Nolan let go and backed away, lowering his gun.

"You're nuts. Get back to work." He returned to leaning on the wall, occasionally aiming the gun in her direction. Molly ignored him. The others wouldn't look at her.

Measure, stir, pack.

Blue stay away, don't let your mom lose you a second time.

CHAPTER 22
Thursday, May 16

Blue woke with a start, sun shining into his eyes.

"What time is it?"

"Getting close to noon." Sam looked up at the sun. "Feeling better?"

"You should have woken me earlier." Blue rolled to his feet, then checked his boots, dry enough. He pulled them on over a pair of socks from his bag.

"Won't do anyone good if you fall over from exhaustion." Sam tossed him a granola bar. "Eat up, then tell me what your plan is."

"Plan?" Blue munched on the bar.

"How do you plan to find Molly? How are you going to get her away from guys who individually can beat you to a pulp?" Sam leaned forward. "Unless you have an arsenal in that bag of yours, you'll need a plan."

"Cause trouble, then follow it." Blue retied his laces, then double knotted them.

"How many fights can you win?" Sam frowned at him.

"I don't plan on doing the fighting." Blue stretched then peered at Sam. "I'll need your help."

"I'd be even worse at fighting than you."

"You won't be fighting, you'll be talking." Nervous energy made Blue pace around, waving his hands. "You have a cell phone, call 911 and tell them you saw someone dragging a girl into that house Molly escaped from. That will get a response and they'll want to check the house, with a suspicion of a crime in progress they won't need a search warrant."

"How will that find Molly?" Sam sighed. "You already said she probably wasn't in that place."

"If the police show up, someone will tell Tad, if he isn't in the place himself. Either Tad or one the gang will want to look at the damage. While the police are watching the house, I'll be watching for whoever is watching the police."

"I guess it's better than nothing." Sam pushed himself up. "You'll have to walk me past the place so I can give a convincing description of it."

"I'll lead you to the street, then tell you which house it is. If I get too close, it could all fall apart."

They headed toward Tranquille. Blue stopped at the Salvation Army and bought a new shirt and camo jacket along with a hat. He described the house and told Sam to look for the broken window. Movement caught his attention.

Was that Hank?

"Hold off for a bit." Blue stopped Sam. "I'm going to see if I can chase someone down."

***

Hank leaned against the wall, panting. Had Blue seen him? He didn't wait around to find out. The old guy thought a new jacket would hide him, but he moved like he was ready to kill. Hank's blood ran cold.

He has to know you screwed him over. Hank peered around the corner to see Blue crossing the street toward him. He took off at a run. It was the old guy's fault. If he'd just helped Hank, none of this would have happened. Hank would be gone, and things would be fixed.

He jogged through the streets without thinking until he realized he was leading Blue straight to the garage. That would mess up his chances good. Hank waited until Blue appeared at the end of the block, then changed directions to put distance between him and the garage. He'd lose the old fart, then double back.

Past the water park, not yet cleaned and ready for the summer, a few people played with dogs. Hank slowed a bit. Maybe he could turn the tables on Blue. It didn't take much to put a scared look on his face.

"Hey, you gotta help me." Hank puffed, dramatically leaning on his knees. "Some old guy is after me, was yelling and waving a knife. Something about me robbing him." He pointed back where Blue would walk around the corner any second.

"How do we know you didn't rob him?" The man with the big yellow dog frowned, but the woman with the smaller black dog pulled out her phone.

"I'll call the police, anyway."

Hank rolled his eyes. That wouldn't help him. Then Blue stepped out onto the street. Hank shouted and backed away.

"That's him." He took off at a run.

See how you deal with that.

***

Blue stepped back behind the bushes. *Smart kid.* Blue headed back up the street, dumping the jacket and hat. If the dog walkers did give a description, it would be only the surface clothes. Tad or Hank would spot him without them, but Hank had made him immediately, anyway.

He walked in the general direction that Hank had taken watching for movement which looked too sudden. Twice he thought he might have spotted the kid, but each time he was wrong.

Back to plan A.

Blue cut across toward Tranquille. He'd meet up with Sam and follow his original idea. Hank was talking to some woman in a bright pink jacket. With a shock, Blue recognized Hannah. She looked around suspiciously, but finally shrugged and strutted away. Hank turned and his eyes went wide before he broke into a sprint, leading Blue across Tranquille and through industrial buildings and stores.

After searching around in circles for too long, Blue admitted he'd lost Hank and maybe blown his chance to find Molly. The kid had to be involved in her disappearance. He'd all but threatened to turn her over if Blue didn't pony up to get him out of the gang.

The kid must think a bit of money and a new city would solve all his problems. Right now, Blue didn't care. He had to back off and pick up the trail again when Hank calmed down. Sam would have to wait before siccing the cops on the house. If Hannah had been sent with a warning, the police showing up would make things worse.

Blue swore at himself. He should have stuck with his original plan, as thin as it was. He walked north to where he'd left Sam waiting. It had to have been hours. Hopefully Sam hadn't given up and gone home.

Sam waited in the Tim Horton's sipping at a coffee.

"Any luck?" He lifted an eyebrow.

"Nothing." Blue bought a coffee, then sat. "The kid can run faster than me, and he's smart enough to think ahead."

"I guess it was worth a try." Sam shrugged and added more sugar to his mug.

"Should have stayed with the plan." Blue blew on his coffee.

"What's next?"

"We drink our coffee and hope I can pick up the trail when Hank thinks he's shaken me."

When his coffee was almost gone, two cruisers whipped past the Timmies lights on.

"That doesn't look good." Blue stood. "I'm going to go see what's happening."

"I'll wait for you here." Sam went to the counter to order another coffee as Blue left.

He wove through the streets, then looked down the back alley. A cop car blocked it, lights flashing blue and red in the growing twilight. Two more parked in the front. A big man wrestled against the cops even in cuffs. Hannah stood, arms wrapped around herself, with a woman cop beside her. An officer walked out of the house talking on the radio.

Hannah bolted down the street. The woman cop gave chase and tackled her. Two more officers helped bring the screaming and fighting woman back to the cars. They cuffed her as two more cars arrived. Whatever had happened, it had caused more ruckus than Blue had dared hope, but in the gloom, he could see the outlines of rubberneckers, but not make out any faces.

"I've had it with that place." An old man leaned on a stick beside Blue. "Them two were going at it hammer and tongs on the front lawn, screaming, swearing. She gave as good as she got from that brute. I called it in, been waiting for a chance for years. Maybe this will close the place down."

Yet more police entered the house. Lights went on as they searched room by room. Nobody moved in the other half of the side-by-side. Then the door burst open and a man ran out, pants around his knees, trying to run and pull them up at the same time. Lights shone from windows as. shouting from inside grew louder. Shortly after, officers led more men out, then a trio of girls in various stages of undress. None of them looked like Molly, and Blue didn't know whether to be relieved or disappointed.

For now, he had nothing better to do than watch the show and hope something caught his eye.

***

Hank watched the cops from a distance, chewing on his knuckles. Tad would kill him. Didn't matter it was Hannah's fault for picking a fight, Hank would get the blame. He always got the blame.

All he'd wanted was Hannah to let Tad know the old man was on the prowl, instead she'd brought every cop in Kamloops down on them.

The only thing to do now was go to the garage and try to stay away from Tad.

Wherever he was. Hank couldn't recall when he'd seen him last, not since they'd brought Molly in to pack. Maybe the boss was keeping him busy away from the place. Even Hank could see Tad was tough, but dumb as a bag of hammers.

Hank walked away, hands in his pockets, trying to look casual.

At the garage, he knocked twice, then twice again before unlocking the door and walking in. The place stank of stale sweat. Molly and the other packers moved mechanically.

The boxes of baggies leaned haphazardly against the wall. Hank straightened them.

"My work isn't good enough?" Nolan didn't look happy.

"The boss was very fussy about how they were to look." Hank shrugged, then turned back to count them. "We're almost done. What happened to her?" He checked the pulse of the girl on the floor. Weak, but there.

"Fell down, I moved her out of the way." Nolan stretched. "Shove her in the RV."

Hank grunted as he dragged the girl to the other room, then hoisted her into the RV. Nolan dragged Molly and the other girl into the RV and tripped a latch at the end of the double bed and the mattress lifted up revealing a hiding place. He shoved them down into the box, lined on all sides with foam, then dumped the unconscious one on top of them. The mattress clicked back into place. Muffled screams came from the box.

"Scream all you want." Nolan kicked the side of the bed. "No one will hear you, what do you think this thing is for?" He laughed, then pushed Hank out, locking the door behind them. "Don't want you sneaking in to get any."

Back in the other room, Nolan dropped piles of cash in front of the four remaining packers. "Take it and get out. Don't even whisper about what you were doing. I'll hear and come looking for you." The four nodded, snatched up the money and headed for the door. One man grabbed up the black jacket Molly had worn when they caught her.

"Tad will be back soon. He texted me he's arranged to sell these two girls, and he's bringing back a couple of new ones. The boss doesn't want him distracted by that skinny bitch." Nolan leaned against the wall.

"One thing, Nolan." Hank swallowed, but if the old guy came around and they weren't watching, it would be worse. "This old guy spotted me and chased me all over the place. Molly's friend."

"Shit." Nolan frowned. "You stay here and wait for the boss. I'll go watch for this old guy."

Hank tried to lean against the wall, looking as cool as Nolan, but his palms sweated. Would the boss really let him go? He'd done everything she wanted. If Tad learned he'd brought in the girl and not told him, he'd probably kill Hank there and then. If he'd heard about the cat house, he'd be in a pissy mood already.

Damn, but he needed to get out of town. Hank looked around, then slipped a few of the baggies left on the table into his pocket. It was still covered with piles of powder, now half blended together, more powder covered the floor.

Well, shit, I'm not cleaning it up. He gave up on being cool and paced around the garage.

***

Molly lay in the tiny space. Jice's breathing was barely audible. Tiff was sobbing. Crying wouldn't get them out of here. The air was already stuffy, but if they used this to transport girls, they wouldn't want corpses at the other end.

She'd got out of the punishment room because who knows how many girls had fought against the cuffs, weakening the bed. Maybe the same thing would happen here. Better to die trying to escape than take this ride west.

Kicking the board made little sound because of the foam. There wasn't much room, but if Molly lay on her side, she could draw her leg up further to kick. She grunted with each kick, and when one leg tired, she rolled over and used the other one.

Time passed, counted by the number of times she had to stop and rest, roll over and start again. In the dark, stuffy space Molly focused on only one thing, breaking the box. She had no idea of when the sound changed from a muffled thud to a thud with a squeak. Molly renewed her attack. Something would give. It had to.

Then the side of the box moved. She felt it give, then push back. Molly gathered all her remaining strength and aimed a kick at the place.

Her foot pushed through a gap, then the boards closed on her ankle like a bear trap. Screws dug into her skin. Molly couldn't pull her foot back or push it forward. Pain and frustration welled up in her and she screamed until her throat hurt.

***

Blue watched the circus until he couldn't stand it anymore. The officers were methodical, careful, and no help to him at all. The sky had clouded over and it started to rain.

He needed something definite to grab their attention. Damn, he shouldn't have lost Hank. It was like the kid had suddenly got a message and changed tactics.

Or he got too close to a place he didn't want Blue knowing about.

Blue walked along the street toward where Hank had suddenly moved in a new direction. Not toward somewhere, but away. It had to be that. Panic would make him run to a safety, but then he calmed down, realized what he was doing.

The street grew quiet. Not that late yet, but the rain kept people inside. The blue glow of TV's told him few people were looking out the windows.

A man in a black jacket ducked through the overgrown yard of an abandoned house. He looked around, then pulled at a basement window. White showed through the back of the jacket, as if someone had cut the material. Blue headed toward the man, catching up just as the window came open.

"Where did you get the jacket?" Now that he was closer, it was obviously his; the leather sliced open at the back and on one arm.

"Picked it up," the man said and crossed his arms as if to hold on to it tighter.

"Show me where, and you can keep it." Blue lifted the man to his feet with a grip on the collar.

"Fine." The man walked back onto the street and glanced around.

164

"Try to run and you'll regret it." Blue made the words a growl.

He led Blue through the rain until he pointed at a cinderblock building.

"There."

Blue let him go. The building looked deserted, dark. But a black truck parked across the street from it. Didn't Molly say Tad drove a black truck? He walked over to put a hand on it. Still warm, even in the rain, so it hadn't been here long.

Blue circled around to come at the building through the back alley where the shadows were thicker. Creeping up to a door, he felt for a knob, but only found a padlock. Back against the wall, Blue slid along to a window. Was that a slight glow coming from the edge?

A blow slammed his head into the block wall and Blue staggered, trying to recover and get his hands up. A fist connected with his stomach, driving the air out of him, he fell to the ground. A kick landed on his back and something trickled from the stitches holding the cut closed.

"The boss is coming; we need to let her in." Tad's voice was low.

"What do we do with him?" Nolan asked.

"Bring him in with us. We'll inject him and dump him somewhere. Just one more dead junkie."

Nolan hoisted Blue up and they walked to the end of the building near the street. Tad went first, unlocked the door, then Nolan followed with Blue. Even if someone had been looking out their windows, they probably wouldn't have noticed anything.

Tad pulled on a chain opening the big door enough for an expensive-looking car to drive in and park to one side of a battered RV. He closed the door and threw a bolt to secure it. Blue gathered himself to escape, then Nolan threw him onto the floor and systematically kicked him until Blue hung on the edge of unconsciousness.

"Bring him into the other room and watch him." The woman climbing out of the car looked familiar even through the blood dripping into Blue's eyes. "We need to organize the product for our dealers, they'll be looking for us in the morning. Right?" Her tone suggested the only correct answer was 'yes.'.

Nolan grabbed one of Blue's feet and dragged him toward another space with light shining from gaps on either side of the building. In the room, Tad kicked Blue against a wall with a stack of what looked like flour bags. Nolan stood on one side and Tad on the other. Hank by a stack of boxes on the end wall.

"You caught him." Hank looked either triumphant or like he wanted to be sick. Blue was too sore to care.

CHAPTER 23

Hank wiped his hand on his jeans. Seeing the packers get paid off made him think he too might see some cash. He glanced at the boss, but she focused on the mess on the table.

"That is a waste." She didn't quite flick the powder on the table. "You should have kept them until it was all used up."

"Hank can finish it up." Tad frowned. "He was the one in charge."

"Why on earth would you leave a kid in charge of something so important?" The boss pointed at Tad. "You are the leader of this group. Everything is your responsibility."

The look Tad shot at Hank didn't bode well for his future. Hank wiped his hands again and fought the nausea in his gut. This is why he wanted out. To get away from assholes like Tad, who blamed him for everything.

"We'll deal with it." Nolan sounded bored. "We gotta load those boxes to go to the distribution sites."

"Go get your truck. We'll put them in the toolbox."

"There's a box of papers in the trunk of my car." The boss nodded at Hank. "Go get them."

He walked around the far side of the table from Tad and Nolan. The lid of the car's trunk was open. The box weighed a ton, but he hoisted it up, carefully closing the trunk before returning to the other room.

"Put it there on the floor." The boss ordered, tapping her toe. "Open it, then put a stack of those flyers on top of each box, then tape them up."

"We don't have any tape." Hank flicked his knife open and cut the heavy box.

"Why not?" The toe was going faster.

"I have some in my truck." Nolan sauntered out. Hank opened a box of drug-filled baggies and stuffed a handful of flyers on top. He adjusted them to make them lie flat.

"Don't fuss, just get it done." Tad growled the words.

"Shut up, Tad. Don't complain at someone doing a proper job."

Tad kicked Blue.

"Restrain yourself." The boss said. "Blood is impossible to get out of concrete."

Hank worked through the boxes, getting each one ready. Eight of them, each one lighter than the one with the flyers, but they might pass a casual inspection.

"Where is that idiot?" Tad moved toward the other room.

"Wait." The boss held up a hand. "Don't want too much movement."

"Fine." Tad leaned against the wall, arms crossed.

Hank couldn't understand why the boss wasn't nervous. Tad looked ready to murder her.

They waited, the boss tapping her toe impatiently, Tad grinding his teeth and glaring at Hank. Hank wanted to hide, to run away and never come back. But he needed the cash to get out of town. He never wanted to see Kamloops again.

Nolan returned holding a roll of tape, a bead of sweat on his face. He tossed the tape to Hank, then returned to lean on the wall by Blue.

"We have visitors."

A man stood in the opening, gun in hand pointed at Nolan. He was one of Tad's bruisers. Across the table from them, three more men walked in. Two of them held guns, one of those a sawed-off shotgun. The last one wore jeans and a t-shirt, but made them look like they cost more than Hank could dream of earning.

"I'm disappointed, Carol," the man looked at the tables and made a face. "You usually aren't that sloppy."

"It is being remedied, Tom." Carol didn't sound at all worried, though three guns were pointed in their direction.

"A new drug, a plan to flood the streets, perhaps to take business away from the south shore." Tom peered at the remaining half dozen bags of pure drugs. "Looks like you plan more than one wave."

"A new product needs to be introduced properly to be successful, then it is important to be able to serve repeat customers."

"Of course." Tom flipped a hand. "I don't have a problem with your process. I do have an issue with being left out of the loop. I too have bills to pay."

"It's business." Carol sounded bored. "Tim Horton's doesn't ask McDonald's permission to bring out a new donut."

"They do take a dim view of someone opening a new Tim Horton's next door to an existing one." Tom sneered at her. "Unlike you, I own a couple of franchises. I know how it works."

For the first time Carol looked angry. "I have no responsibility to you."

"It would have been polite to ask me to invest in your project."

"Take it over you mean." Carol clenched her fists. "You've had your eye on the North Shore since father passed away."

"Not take over." Tom brushed away the suggestion. "Just to work more closely."

"I have no interest in working with you, closely or otherwise."

"Pity." Tom pointed at Hank. "Load those bags in the empty box. My car is outside."

"Don't move." Carol put a hand on his shoulder and her fingernails dug in like claws.

"Be reasonable." Tom smiled. "Don't let this get messy."

"People live on three sides of this place. People we've taken care to avoid upsetting. Gunshots will be reported immediately."

"Perhaps, but by the time the police arrive we'll be gone."

"Obviously you didn't drive past the ongoing situation less than a kilometer from here where I believe there are a half dozen cruisers."

"What do you suggest?" Tom didn't let his smile slip, but his eyes made Hank want to wipe his hands again.

"There are girls in the RV. Take them as a gift. I will sell you half of my supply at wholesale."

"Those are my girls." Tad stepped forward, and all three guns aimed at him.

"Shut up." Carol said. "This is business."

Tad shook a fist at her, then pointed at the bruiser. "You're dead meat."

"Nolan, I assume you have the keys to the RV? Give them to Tom." Carol ignored Tad while the bruiser grinned and waved at Tad to come to him as he put his gun in his belt behind him.

***

Blue took stock of his injuries while they argued. He didn't expect to make it out alive, but perhaps he'd get a chance to do some damage before they got him.

If only he'd called in the police to investigate the garage instead of doing it himself. And he was the one who kept saying it wasn't like the movies. Too late now. He'd failed Molly. Dying held no fear for him. More than once the last few years he'd seriously considered ending the charade.

Some foggy pigheadedness kept him waking up and going through the motions of living. Then Molly had shaken all that up. Suddenly he made a difference to someone.

The vision of the red room swept over him. The murdered children, the dead father, but this time the red faded away. The kids stood hand in hand, looking at him sadly.

"You didn't kill us." The girl said.

"I failed you." Blue reached out to her.

"How?" She tilted her head. "Can you read minds? Are you a superhero?"

"But..."

The boy shook his head. "Daddy broke. You couldn't save us."

"Sometimes, bad things happen." The girl took Blue's hand, and warmth flooded through him. "Take care of your own soul. It's time to let us go. Don't let our death kill you."

They faded away.

Tad was yelling about his girls.

"Molly." Blue whispered. As Tad charged past him, Blue spun on the floor and kicked Tad's leg. Tad crashed into the tables, knocking them over and sending a cloud of powder into the air. He rolled to his feet and slashed at Tom with a knife.

The shotgun roared. Tad fell back with a bloody hole through him.

"Shit." Carol reached into her purse as Tom's men lifted their weapons. Nolan snatched his gun from behind him and shot the bruiser as he reached for his own gun.

Blue stayed low, but without the tables he was a clear target. Desperately he threw a bag from behind him at the man with the shotgun. The blast of the gun blew the bag into powder and it became hard to see in the room. Blue threw more bags as bullets hit the wall beside him. Nolan grunted and fell to the floor.

Blue needed to get out of this room filled with deadly bullets. He could still see outlines of men on the other side. A bag in each fist, he slammed his hands together, creating a huge cloud of powder. The gunshots continued as he rolled away toward Nolan and fished in the man's pockets. He grabbed the keys and for a moment the gun on the floor tempted him, but he wouldn't do any good adding more random shots to the room.

Rolling out through the gap, blood stuck to him, making him red and white. A single harsh bulb illuminated the other half of the garage. Carol's car parked on the wall nearest him. The RV sat in the middle over an oil pit, and past it the door out of the garage.

A man dragged another out of the room. He saw Blue and his gun came up. The cloud of powder in the air was much thinner here, and he had a clear shot. Blue scrambled for shelter, but didn't have a chance.

***

Hank almost wet his pants when Tad died with a hole through him. As often as he'd dreamed of killing someone, and threatened to with his knife, when it came to it, he more ran away oftenthan fought.

He huddled against the wall, screaming in fear. All he'd wanted was enough money to escape and start over. How did he end up here?

Because I'm chicken shit. Hank wiped powder from his eyes. Blue had gone crazy throwing bags of cornstarch like they would actually make a difference. Carol's gun fired near his head until she coughed and fell to her knees. Blood rain out a hole in her side.

"Shit." She lifted the gun and started shooting again. Bullets came back, making tiny holes in her blouse which leaked blood. Then a bullet hit Hank.

Breathing was impossible. The pain ran through him like a fire. He coughed and tried to get air into his lungs, but they wouldn't work.

He fell to the floor. *Kill them all.* It was impossible; he was dying. Then he remembered Nolan's face when he took the lighter away from the smoker. Hank reached into his pocket and pulled it out. He never knew if he succeeded in lighting it.

***

The blast shook the building and blew out the windows. Flames engulfed the men across from Blue. Heat scorched his own back. Blue lurched to his feet and staggered to the RV. He unlocked the door and slid over to the driver's seat.

Putting the key in the ignition was harder than it should have been. His hand shook, and his vision faded in an out. Finally, it found the right place, and the engine roared to life, barely audible over the sound of the fire raging through the building. Blue put the vehicle into reverse and floored the gas pedal.

The RV drove backwards into the big garage door. The shock threw Blue back against the seat, then forward into the steering wheel. Cold air blew in through the broken window beside him. He groped for some way to move to find Molly, but nothing remained of his strength. Leaning against the door, he closed his eyes.

CHAPTER 24

Constable Madoc sighed and looked over at Hannah, who was still alternating between almost comatose depression and frenetic rage. The big man had been taken away already, but she still fixated on the fight with him. Something about him not taking her seriously. Night had arrived, and the flashing lights of the cruisers lent the scene a surreal look. Floodlights illuminated the front of the house; more lit the back as she kept up her babble.

"I told him someone was about to make trouble, but he laughed and said he could handle it. I had to beat it into him." Hannah fought against the handcuffs, kicking the back of the seat in the cruiser, screaming her complaints the whole time.

"When he got into the car to go to holding," Constable Singh leaned against the car, backup in case she broke loose. "I swear he looked relieved to be out of her reach."

"I don't doubt it." Madoc closed the door, cutting off the woman's tirade. "Don't know if she's on anything or just like this. I'm going to talk to the other women."

"I'll watch to be sure she doesn't hurt herself."

"Thanks, I owe you."

Madoc headed over to where three young women, girls really, stood huddled in blankets.

"How are you doing?"

"I didn't get paid yet, and I'm dying for a smoke." The oldest-looking woman glared at Madoc.

Madoc waved John over.

"Could you fetch the courtesy pack from the car?"

"Sure thing, boss."

"Cute, what's he like?" The girl batted her eyes.

"Very detail oriented, observant. His boyfriend claims he's a great cook too."

"Oh well." The woman pulled the blanket tighter. "When do we get our clothes back?"

"They are processing the house as a crime scene. It could take a while."

"Crap. I have money in my jeans pocket. Don't want that disappearing." The youngest one gazed up at the window.

"Yeah right, Kat." The third one bumped her hip into Kat. "Like they'll believe that." She had pants and a bra and wasn't shy about dropping the blanket to let her assets shine.

"How much?" Madoc pulled out her notebook.

"Uh…" Kat stared up at the window. "There was a twenty, and three fives, no two, I bought coffee with one, then a pile of change."

Madoc wandered over to an officer holding a clipboard.

"One of the girls is worried about money in her jeans pocket."

"Right, let me look." He flipped through a couple of pages. "Yup, here it is. Jeans, panties, bra, t-shirt, Money. Two twenties, two fives and twelve fifty in change. We probably won't hold it as evidence. The men were warned and turned loose, except one who had an active warrant."

"Thanks."

When Madoc returned to the trio, John was handing out cigarettes and lighting them for the women. He had them giggling.

"Well?" Kat lifted her chin.

"You were off, there were two twenties." Madoc smiled slightly. "Chances are it will be released to you before you go."

"Before we go?" The older one stepped up close to Madoc. "The men are already gone, but we're still here. What gives?"

"You are not being charged," Madoc held the woman's eyes, "but we have a responsibility to make sure you're safe."

"Safe?"

"That's right. If you aren't here of your own free will, the people holding you could be charged."

"Would I have to testify?" Kat's eyes widened.

"Perhaps, it would depend on the Crown and whether they make a deal with—"

The explosion made Madoc spin to see an immense column of flame reaching for the sky.

"That doesn't look good." Kat said.

"No shit." The older one had lost her blanket.

"John, please take over here." Madoc's gut knotted as she ran. The officer in charge of the scene was already reporting the explosion to dispatch.

"My cruiser is free." Madoc yelled. The officer nodded without stopping his report. She dashed back to the cruiser, took a deep breath and drove in the direct of the fire. The column had shrunk, but it still lit the night. She pulled up in front of the building just as another cruiser parked back in the alley. The other officer was already reporting the location and description of the blaze to dispatch, so Madoc ran over to the RV crashed into a black pickup, blocking the road in front of her, what was left of a garage door wrapped around it.

When she opened the driver's side door, a body fell out on her. Madoc reacted fast enough to keep the man from landing on his head.

Another cruiser arrived on the far side of the RV.

"Girls...back," the man said. His face was powder white and blood red, but Madoc recognized Blue. Molly could be one of those in the back of the RV.

Constable McCall ran over with a first aid kit from her car.

"I've got this." She dropped to her knees to assess the injuries. Madoc remembered McCall was also a fully trained paramedic.

Madoc tried the door to the RV, but it was locked. She slipped past McCall and Blue to take the keys from the ignition and ran back to try them on the door. The third attempt was successful. After pulling out her flashlight, Madoc yanked the door open, but nothing moved inside. She climbed in, shining her light, almost screaming when it lit up a severed foot.

Not severed - sticking out from under the bed. Madoc tried to lift the mattress, but it wouldn't budge. She felt for a catch, found it, and the mattress and board lifted slightly. Madoc heaved it up and hydraulic lifts held it in place.

Molly lay pale and unmoving, her foot through a gap in the boards.

"Need rescue in the RV." Madoc spoke into her mic.

"They are arriving on the scene, will advise."

While she waited, Madoc checked the pulse of all three girls. Two had a heartbeat, though Molly's was weak.

"What's the status?" A firefighter climbed into the RV carrying a rescue box. Madoc stepped back and pointed to where Molly's foot was caught. The man felt for a pulse in her foot. "You know how long she's been like this?"

"No idea. Sorry."

"I think we still have blood flow through the foot. We'll risk freeing her. The ambulance will be here soon." He opened the box and pulled out a tool he used to spread the gap until her foot dropped free. "Blood's red, that's good." He wrapped the foot, and Molly whimpered.

"You're going to be fine." The firefighter shone a flashlight on himself, then Madoc. The paramedics arrived as the firefighter was checking Molly for other injuries. They lifted her out as Madoc checked the rest of the interior, finding nothing important. She followed the people carrying the other living girl out into rain that had started up again.

Sirens wailed as ambulances came and went.

"Your guy at the front is hanging in there. He's got a good chance. Only two gunshot wounds and neither hit anything major. Mostly shock. Someone gave him a hell of a beating." McCall nodded at Madoc, then went to deal with the gathering crowd. More firetrucks arrived and hoses sprayed the fire. It looked like it wouldn't take long to control, and it hadn't spread past the one building.

Hours later, the firefighters were able to enter the building. They came out pale.

"Bodies all over," One came over to report to Madoc. "Three in the room closer to us, five in the other. Might be gunshot wounds on them, hard to tell." He pointed to the RV. "Those ones were lucky, the wall between the rooms protected them from the shock wave."

As the scene turned from a fire into a crime scene, the firetrucks drove away while officers strung tape around the building. McCall and another officer were set watching the scene. Madoc drove up to the hospital, informed dispatch, then went looking for Molly, Blue and the other girl.

"Molly and the man are in surgery." The nurse told Madoc, but you can talk to Tiff.

She found Tiff curled up into a ball on the bed.

"My mom and dad are going to kill me." She wouldn't look at Madoc.

"Do you want me to call them?"

"The nurse already did." Tiff sniffled. "I'll be grounded forever."

After a commotion on the other side of the curtain, a man and woman ran into the room.

"Tiffany, are you okay?" The woman brushed hair off her daughter's face.

"Officer, is my daughter in trouble?"

"I can't comment on the investigation." Madoc handed him a card. "I am here in a support role and at this time she's not under arrest. She is a material witness, so I'll need to know where she is until the case is cleared."

The man peered at the card. "Mental health assessment and support. What is this about?"

"Police often encounter situations where mental health is part of the issue. My job is to help sort out those situations in a way which keeps everyone safe." She gave him another card. "This is for Victim Services; they have resources that will help you and your daughter."

"Thank you."

"I want to talk to the cop." Tiff sat up, leaning against her mom. "You guys might as well stay and listen too. This guy told us we could make some quick money. Jice was all over it, I went along with her..."

The story of their time in the garage came out, her parents growing paler with each word, but neither one interrupted.

"Are you going to arrest me now?" Tiff looked up at Madoc, her face wet with tears.

"No." Madoc put her notebook away. "You'll need to make an official statement at the station, and you can bring a lawyer if you want, but it sounds to me like you were coerced and held against your will. That makes you a victim, not a criminal."

"Oh." Tiff hung her head. "Jice is dead, isn't she? If I'd argued, held her back..."

"I won't say this will be easy." Madoc crouched to look Tiff in the eyes. "You must deal with what happened but saying 'what if' won't help. Phone the number on that card. Get some help, let your parents help you."

"Can we take her home?" Tiff's dad put a hand on his daughter's head.

"As soon as the doctor clears her. Just don't leave town."

Madoc checked with the nurse to learn that Molly was out of surgery and awake and asking for her. She followed the nurse to a room where Molly sat on the bed, looking even thinner and younger in the hospital gown and an IV in her arm.

"I thought I dreamed seeing you." Molly scrubbed her face.

"I'm glad I found you." Madoc pulled a chair over. "How's the foot?"

"Sore. The doctor said something about tissue damage, but at least it's still attached."

"You'll need to make an official statement later, but do you want to tell me what happened?"

Molly's story matched Tiff's except for her abduction instead of being lured by easy money. She gave a description of the other people who packed drugs and were paid off.

"Have you heard from Blue?" Molly studied her hands.

"He's in surgery," Madoc said. "Somehow he found you and got you out. He told me where to look."

Molly put her head in her hands and sobbed. "It's all my fault."

"Blue cares about you enough to have gone looking for you. I doubt he blames you."

"He just found his mom again too." Molly lifted her head to look at Madoc. "You have to call her."

"Do you have her number?"

"It's on Sam's phone, but I don't know where he'll be. But if you look up unHooked, it's an agency in Alberta that Blue's mom runs for girls getting off the street."

"I'll do what I can." Madoc stood and put the chair back. "Try to get some rest. I will let the nurses know to keep you posted about Blue."

She ended up telling the nurse Molly was Blue's daughter to get them to agree to keep her in the loop. Madoc headed back to her office in the station on Battle St. She had a few hours to do paperwork before her shift ended.

The number for uHooked went to an answering machine. So did the cell phone. The woman at the emergency number only said the boss was out of town. Madoc shrugged to loosen her shoulders, then opened a file on the computer.

CHAPTER 25
Friday, May 17

Sun glared in a stripe across a white ceiling. A machine beeped and aches through his body told the story. A hospital room. His mouth was so dry he couldn't swallow, and his body refused to move.

"Easy." Someone put a straw in his mouth, and he sucked in lukewarm tap water. It loosened his throat, and he swallowed.

Imagine feeling such accomplishment just for swallowing. Blue's lips quirked. He couldn't get his eyes to focus, then he couldn't keep them open.

***

Molly put the water glass down and wiped the tears from her face. She'd never been so scared seeing his still body after surgery. They'd said it went well, but she couldn't trust it until he'd opened his eyes. The nurses said to get him to drink as much as possible.

Her foot rested on another chair. If it touched the floor, she'd be banished back to her own room. The pills they gave her had worn off, but the pain anchored her in the moment, telling her it was real. She'd woken in the dark after the cop left and screamed until the nurses came running.

Guess I'll need a nightlight for a while.

Blue's face was bruised, and bandages covered cuts on his cheeks and forehead. Some ribs were cracked, he had taken a bullet through the side of his abdomen, and another in the leg. A centimeter or two in the wrong direction and either would have killed him.

"How is our patient?" A nurse came into the room.

"He woke up for a few seconds and I gave him a drink."

"Excellent." The nurse took notes from the machines and adjusted the IV. "He'll probably be in and out a few times before he completely wakes up."

"That's all right. I'm not going anywhere."

"He's lucky to have a daughter like you." The nurse took Molly's pulse and blood pressure. "Any pain? The doctor has said we can give you something for it."

"I'm good." Molly wiped her eyes again. "It's reminding me this is real."

"Let me know if reality gets too hard." The nurse smiled at her.

His daughter. If only... Molly had fought to keep her face straight when the doctor showed up to tell her what her father's condition was. Whoever made the mistake, Molly wasn't going to correct it. For a while, until Blue woke up, she'd live the fantasy she had a father who gave a damn about her.

There was a time she'd have been restless after only a few minutes of sitting still, but Molly watched over Blue, giving him a drink when he'd wake for a moment, the time precious, not a punishment.

All his injuries, they were her fault. She'd latched onto him to protect herself, then because he'd treated her with kindness, then because...

Molly left the tears on her face. She couldn't admit it, even in her thoughts. Something she didn't think was still possible for her.

"Hello, you must be Molly." A woman with grey hair in a comfortable pair of grey pants and emerald green blouse came into the room and pulled up a chair.

"You the social worker?" Molly asked. They'd said something about that. She tugged at the robe covering the hospital gown. This woman didn't need to see the marks of her addiction.

"I am a social worker." The woman smiled and sighed as she sat down. "But not the one you may be expecting. I arrived at the airport and had a conversation with a man named Sam. He suggested the police might know what had happened to Blue. The police directed me here. Imagine my surprise when the hospital staff told me Blue's daughter was sitting with him." Her smiled broadened. "That would make me your grandmother."

"Grandmother?" Molly's jaw dropped open. "You're Blue's mom? I'm sorry, I'll leave now."

The woman put a hand on Molly's leg.

"You will stay here." Though that smile still shone, tears glistened on the woman's cheeks. She pulled her chair closer to Molly and wrapped warm arms around her. All the guilt and hope, fear and love formed a tangled ball in Molly's chest, then exploded. She sobbed, holding tight to this stranger.

When the crying spell passed, Molly sat up, her face hot. That green blouse had a large damp spot on one shoulder. The woman didn't appear to care. She handed Molly a tissue.

"Life can get overwhelming at times like this." The woman dried her own face, then tucked the tissue in her sleeve. "All we can do is let it out, and hope people will understand." She looked at Blue. "I couldn't wait in my office for a phone call, so here I am."

"Molly." Blue's voice wasn't more than a whisper, but she instantly focused on him.

"Blue, have a drink first." She put the straw in his mouth.

"Thank God you're all right." Blue turned his head enough to meet her eyes. "I was so afraid I'd got you in a mess and lost you." His hand slid across the sheets. Molly took it in hers.

"It wasn't your fault." Molly squeezed his hand. In this moment the two of them were alone in the world.

"Not yours either." Blue's eye's narrowed. "Stuff happens, then we pick up the pieces and learn to live with the scars."

"Someone told the staff I was your daughter." Molly whispered and hung her head.

"I can live with that." Blue shook her hand. "After what we've been through, might as well be family."

"Blue, I..." Molly had to stop and take a deep breath, there wasn't enough air to say what she wanted to. "I love you. I so much want to be your daughter but..."

"Love you too, kiddo." Blue smiled. "We aren't the usual thing, but we'll work it out." His eyes closed. "Sorry, Molly, I'm so tired."

Molly held his hand as his breathing slowed and evened out. Whole new spaces opened inside her she'd never known were there.

A nurse came in, pushing a big chair.

"This is a recliner. It might be more comfortable. You'll want to get some rest yourself." He helped Molly hop over to the recliner. She curled up, and he put a blanket over her. Someone tucked it in tighter.

Her grandmother brushed a hand over Molly's cheek. "Go ahead a sleep. It's my turn to watch." She went to sleep holding the word '*grandmother*' like a precious gem.

***

Blue opened his eyes to a dimly lit room.

"Need to use the washroom."

"I'll call the nurse." Someone patted his hand. Not Molly.

The nurse came in and pulled the curtain around and helped with the embarrassing task. He checked Blue's vitals then opened the curtain again.

"I'll leave you two alone."

Blue turned his head and saw a familiar face.

"Mom." He blinked. "How long have you been here?"

"Long enough to meet your daughter." His mom pulled her chair closer. "She's been deeply wounded by life, but you know that."

"I'm sorry." Blue couldn't get out more than those two words, so inadequate for the pain he'd caused her.

"I know, and I forgive you." She lifted his hand to kiss it. "Did you think I would find my son after all this time, then lose him because of my anger?"

"But..."

"I was angry." His mom looked at a spot on the wall. "There were days I wished they would find your body because that would hurt less than not knowing. Other days I hoped you were out there healing and finding happiness. My heart just about stopped when I recognized your voice on my answering service. Poor Sam must have been overwhelmed by my attempts to contact you through him."

"He wasn't worried about it. Sam's... well, Sam."

"We had a pleasant chat while you and Molly were sleeping. He's glad to hear you are both all right."

"Thanks, Mom." Blue turned his head to look at her. More grey in her hair, more lines, but her strength and kindness still shone through.

"How are Jill and Keith?" His absence would have hurt his siblings as much as his mother.

"Very excited to know you're alive and doing well."

"I'll call them later." Blue closed his eyes. "I'm not sure I can handle it yet."

"When you're ready, they'll be there." His mom leaned forward. "I let your father know too."

"You talked to dad?" Blue's eyes went wide in shock.

"I don't like him much, but he's your father and should know you're okay."

"That's a conversation I'm really not ready to have."

"Then wait until you're ready."

***

A knock at the door made Blue look up as Constable Madoc walked into the room.

"Good to see you looking better." She smiled and took a chair.

"We will leave you to talk." Blue's mom stood up and shook Molly awake, then signalled to follow her out of the room.

"I've already talked to Molly about what happened to her." Madoc took out her notebook and pen. "Now it's your turn."

"I've been expecting a visit." Blue tried to get more comfortable in the bed, but his wounds pulled and ached. "I'm glad it's you."

"I'm honoured." Madoc tilted her head. "How about you start at the beginning and just tell me the story in your own words."

"Molly didn't want to leave Tad to run roughshod over the North Shore, so we were trying to get a couple of juicy tips to put a spoke in his wheel."

"That's really a job for the police."

"No one knows that better than me, but we hear things you never do. All we needed was those tidbits. Then Molly got snatched a second time."

"A second time?" Madoc's hand froze over her notebook.

"The first time put me in the hospital, one of your colleagues took my statement. They said they would put out the word that she was missing."

"I'm guessing you didn't hang around to find out." She shook her head. "How did you get her out?"

"I didn't, she broke out on her own." Blue couldn't hide the pride he felt at Molly's determination.

"I haven't heard that story." She made a note. "I will be sure to ask her about it next time we talk."

"After that we moved where we were staying. I thought we were far enough away to be safe, but someone spotted us and picked her up." As Blue told the story, the unreality of what had happened hit him. "I'm not sure I did a single thing right."

"You're alive." Madoc snapped the book shut. "That's one thing. The fire marshal said something about a powder explosion in his report. After I talked to Molly and Tiff, hazmat took over the scene, same as a meth lab. From what they said, the drug was nasty stuff. Think it's still being analyzed somewhere, but there wasn't much left."

"It's a good thing it never made it to the street." Blue rubbed his head. It was aching again. The doctors warned he might have a concussion from the beating.

"I'll say." Madoc leaned back and put her notebook away. "This part is off the record. A few times when I've talked to you, it's been more like talking to another cop than a civilian." She raised an eyebrow.

"I told Molly the story, and I'm guessing Sam heard it at the same time." He stared at his hands, then stumbled through the telling. This time it wasn't as hard, but he still shook uncontrollably by the end.

"I remember hearing about that." Madoc closed her eyes. "I wondered what I would have done."

"Probably dealt with it better than I did." Blue took a shuddering breath. "This stays off the record, but I had a vision while lying in that damned place." He told her about the children telling him to let them go.

191

"Take care of your own soul." Madoc put a hand over her heart. "That's why I'm working Car 40. I knew a young man whose problem was his mental health, not being bad. I wanted to help people like him."

"It can't be easy."

"What is?" Madoc stood and held out her hand. "It's been a privilege to meet you, Blue. Call me if you want to talk."

He shook her hand. The trembling had stopped.

Guess I've taken another step.

***

Molly frowned stubbornly at the hospital social worker.

"I will stay with Blue until he can manage on his own."

"That's all very good, but you both need a place to live." The social worker, she'd told Molly to call her Joan, looked every bit as stubborn as Molly.

"I've talked to Ask Wellness and been calling landlords." Molly clenched her hands. "They all want references, then there is the deposit..." She trailed off.

"Let me talk to some people." The social worker sighed and smiled slightly. "He's lucky to have someone like you to care for him. It will be a few more days before he's released."

"Thank you, Joan." Molly put a hand to her head.

"Go and rest." Joan pointed back toward Blue's room. "First rule of taking care of someone is take care of yourself first."

"I get it."

Molly walked back to the room, using the crutch to take a bit of the weight from her foot. The doctor had referred her to a physiotherapist who gave her a pile of stupid exercises to do. She didn't know if they were helping, but wasn't going to give up on them.

"Well?" Her grandmother smiled at Molly.

"We didn't quite come to blows." Molly plopped into the chair. "She said she'd make some phone calls. That's something."

Blue sat up in the bed "I don't particularly want to convalesce in a nursing home, but we may not have much choice."

"The big hurdle is the deposit and the first month's rent. Nobody wants to let me pay the deposit gradually." Molly sighed and stared up at the ceiling.

Blue smacked his forehead and winced.

"May I borrow your phone, Mom?"

Molly's grandmother handed it over without comment. Blue tapped away at it, chewing his lip at a couple of places. Then started laughing until he held his side.

"I don't believe it." He handed the phone back to his mom, whose eyebrows disappeared into her hair. "They put me on indefinite leave, so they kept paying me. Two year's worth of salary before they gave up. I never was going to touch that money, but I can't remember why. It's worth a bit of humble pie, I can re-apply and maybe get the pension re-instated."

Molly took the phone from her grandmother and almost dropped it.

"That's..." She handed it back to her grandmother. "You can afford a proper apartment and good food."

"You mean, we can." Blue looked at her.

"Blue," Molly held a breath, then let it out in a whoosh. "I've been talking to grandmother, and I want to do her program. I won't leave until you can manage on your own, but..." She stumbled to a stop at the broad grin on Blue's face.

"Mom said it would take a while to do the paperwork and there's a waiting list."

"You knew?" Molly stood up and put her hands on her hips. "And I was dying worrying how to tell you."

"Sorry, kiddo, but it has to be your decision, not feeling like I've pushed you into it. Won't matter where you are, I will still a hundred percent be happy to be your father, but part of that is letting you live your own life."

"Why don't you come with me?" Molly's heart lit up with hope.

"As much as I would like to, this you need to do for yourself. Also, as a residential program, you won't have much chance to see me even if I lived at home. You will can call me whenever you need."

Molly sighed and slumped in the chair.

"Okay, but I'm coming back when I've finished the program." She pouted. "I'll still worry about you living on your own."

"I'm thinking I could ask Sam to share a place with me."

"That's a great idea."

***

Thursday, August 15

Blue joined Sam and Molly at the table. The apartment was in an older complex, but it was near Tranquille and the

North Hills Mall. He'd talked with someone about a trauma group Interior Health ran. It sounded like it wouldn't be horrible.

"This looks great." Sam spooned a large serving of lasagna onto his plate. "How did you learn to cook this?"

"YouTube videos." Molly laughed. "Without them, you'd be eating burnt toast and canned soup."

Blue watched them and smiled, though his heart ached. A space in unhooked had come open and Molly was leaving in the morning. Just as well; any later, he might have broken down and asked her to stay.

"It's going to be fine," he said. "I'll check out those videos and make sure Sam doesn't fade away."

"You do that." Molly grinned, and Blue's heart soared. She would grow and become more independent, but that's what daughters were supposed to do.

CHAPTER 26
Thursday, November 27

Blue sat down at the computer and connected to Molly's call.

"I'm writing a bunch of tests tomorrow." Molly leaned closer to the camera on her laptop. "This is the last bunch and I'll have my high school equivalency."

"What do you want to do after that?" Blue drank in the happiness on her face. Their weekly chats were high points of his life.

"I have no idea." Molly shrugged as if it didn't matter. "I've learned to knit. Isn't that crazy?" She held something up to show him. "This is a scarf. I'm getting better at keeping the tension even. It helps on the bad days."

"Good, maybe I should take it up." Blue grinned at her.

"You get them too?"

"Bad days will happen." Blue leaned forward a bit. "They are like the scars you carry. Never really gone, but most of the time they don't get in the way."

"Makes sense." Molly put the knitting down. "How's Sam?"

"Having a blast in Japan. He sent me pictures; I'll forward them to you."

"Awesome." Molly beamed a smile at him.

"I've arranged time off from the Peer Ambassadors." Blue waited for a moment, watching her face. "I'll be able to join you and your grandmother for Christmas."

Molly jumped up and danced around the room.

"I can't wait."

"Neither can I." Blue put his hand on the screen. Not nearly as good as being able to hug her in person.

Tomorrow he'd put another X on the calendar, counting down the days until he could hold his daughter again.

OTHER BOOKS BY ALEX

Series:

Calliope Books:

Calliope and the Sea Serpent

Calliope and the Royal Engineers

The Third Prince and the Enemy's Daughter

Spruce Bay Books:

Wendigo Whispers

Cry of the White Moose

Disputed Rock

The Belandria Tarot:

The Devil Reversed

The Regent's Reign

The Empire Unbalanced

Stand alone books:

Generation Gap

The Gods Above

Tales of Light and Dark

Like Mushrooms (poetry and photography)

The Heronmaster

Blood and Sparkles, and other stories

Princess of Boring

By the Book

Sarcasm is My Superpower

Playing on Yggdrasil

The Unenchanted Princess

Read short stories and excerpts from his novels at alexmcgilvery.com

Celticfrog Publishing's first Anthology

Mythical Girls

COLUMBIA SMOKE

Read the first Chapter of the next book featuring Blue in Kamloops.

Columbia Smoke

CHAPTER 1
Tuesday, April 10

The smoke alarm shrilled, and Blue sleepily wondered who was making toast in the middle of the night.

"Blue!" Sam banged on the door of his room. "There's a fire, we have to get out."

"Coming." Blue rolled out of bed and pulled clothes on, then packed his computer in its bag and slung it over his shoulder. He slid his phone into his pocket. The reek of smoke attacked his nostrils.

"Get a move on, there's smoke pouring in from the hall." Sam sounded nervous. When Blue opened the bedroom door, he saw Sam clutching a photo album, pictures from his trip to Japan last fall.

"Put it in my bag." Blue held it open.

"We're supposed to leave everything and get out." Sam's eyes were wide.

"We have it now, don't worry about it." Blue yanked the door to the balcony open and checked outside. "No smoke out here." Orange light flickered in the alley and a roaring sound came from the other side of the line of apartments that jutted out from the main building.

Sam joined him and slammed the door behind him. The thing stuck constantly. If they weren't on the third floor, it would be a security risk.

"I'm not climbing down." Though he looked like a somewhat muscular Santa Claus, Sam had just turned sixty-five.

"Me neither." Blue pulled out his cell phone. Only twenty percent battery. He'd left the cord on the desk. The ones for the computer too. Too late to worry about it now. He dialed 911 and reported the fire, but sirens were already wailing as they approached.

The chair they left on the balcony creaked as Sam lowered himself into it. "Might as well be comfortable while we wait."

Smoke drifted from under the balcony door, so Blue leaned against the dividing wall to the next apartment.

When the fire truck rolled up, someone got out and shone a flashlight along the building Blue waved. The firefighters unhooked the ladder and got it extended. One climbed up to Sam and Blue.

"Anyone else in your apartment?"

"We're it." Blue clutched the computer bag, but the firefighter didn't comment. She helped Sam onto the ladder and walked him down, then returned for Blue.

From the ground across the alley, flames lit up the side of the building. Looked like three or four apartments on fire. He shivered and wished he'd thought to grab a jacket. With nothing else to do, Blue stood beside Sam and watched the firefighters work. The crowd on the ground grew, some people dressed like him, others with coats, and still others in pajamas.

People held onto cats, and dogs on leashes. One young woman guarded a stack of what looked like rabbit cages.

"Anybody got a light?" A young man holding a cigarette waved it about.

"Over there." Someone pointed to the fire and people laughed. They clustered together and speculated about the cause, or talked about what they would do now their home was gone. Estimates of days, weeks or even never, made the rounds as they wondered if they'd be able to get back in to the unburned apartments.

"Okay people." A woman with a clipboard waved for attention. "Emergency Services is setting up at the Sportplex on MacArthur Island Park. If you can make your way over there, great. Otherwise a bus will be arriving to take you."

Blue and Sam made it onto the second trip to the arena, a woman pointed them to a room upstairs where they found coffee and cookies waiting for them.

Light was beginning to show in the east when a man in a firefighter's uniform came in and explained what Emergency Services was and how it would work. Inevitably it began with paperwork.

Blue sat down with a volunteer and filled out a form describing his housing situation and what his needs were. There was a voucher for temporary housing and one for clothes from Value Village. They would have a paper to show for meals as well.

Blue was exhausted by the time the bus took them up to a motel on Columbia. This would be a new experience; he'd mostly lived on the North Shore since he came to Kamloops.

The room he would share with Sam had the usual two beds along with a rickety table and chairs, a tiny stove and bar fridge. An odd assortment of pots, pans, dishes and cutlery occupied the cupboards and drawers in the tiny kitchen. An odd musty smell made him remember visiting an old aunt when he was a kid, but it wasn't anything he couldn't deal with.

Blue put the laptop on the table and connected it to the wifi. He'd have to find a power cord for it. Shouldn't be that hard.

He sent Molly a message. *Call me tonight.*

Blue lay on the bed closest to the window and stared at the ceiling. What should he do next? Getting to the North Shore to work with the Peer Ambassadors would be a challenge, but not insurmountable. He'd have to get a bus pass.

Sam walked in the door and plunked onto the other bed.

"My son wants me to fly out to Toronto and stay with them."

"Makes sense to at least visit. You did have a month in Japan with your daughter."

"Yeah." Sam didn't sound convinced. "I don't want to desert you."

"If you were on your own, would you go?" Blue sat up and faced Sam.

"I would." Sam sighed and pulled out his phone, sent a text, then put it back in his pocket. "I will miss you."

"I hope so." Blue grinned at Sam's shocked expression, then they both laughed.

Sam's phone buzzed. He looked at it and rolled his eyes. "Eric has a flight for me leaving tomorrow. He works for Westjet, so he must have pulled some strings."

"I remember he helped you get the flight to Japan too." Blue pushed away the hollow feeling in his chest. Being alone again wasn't an inviting prospect.

"I'll give you my voucher for clothes." Sam shrugged. "It's the least I can do."

"That would be appreciated." Blue lay down again. "I'm going to have a rest, then go up to Value Village."

"It's just up the hill." Sam waved his hand. "An easy walk."

"Nice." Blue closed his eyes

***

"What?" Molly's leaned so close to the computer Blue was afraid she'd bang her head on it. Video chat had its risks.

"A fire. Everybody in the building is out, no one knows for how long, but I expect months at least. Sorry, I didn't even think to grab anything from your room."

"Nothing there I can't stand to lose." Molly put her hands to her head. "I can't get my mind around it."

"I'm still in shock." Blue leaned back. "Sam is off to Toronto tomorrow; his son is paying the airfare. But the upside is I'll have more clothes than I ever had."

"I never knew someone who lived out of one drawer like you."

"Old habits." Blue shrugged.

"Make sure you take care of yourself. I'll be back by the end of June. I've already contacted Thompson Rivers University about their Social Work degree."

"That's great." Blue grinned and his heart lifted. "I'm proud of you."

"Grandma's writing me a reference." Molly frowned. "I'm going to worry about you."

"You're allowed, but only for an hour on alternate Wednesdays. Put it in your calendar."

"Yes, sir." Molly saluted and stuck out her tongue. "I have to go, I've got early shift tomorrow."

"I'm still waiting for a picture of you in your uniform."

"You'll be waiting a long time. Tim Horton's is a nice place to work, but the uniform does nothing for me." Molly laughed and blew him a kiss, then disconnected.

Sam had already gone to bed to be ready for an early flight in the morning. Blue stripped down and crawled under the covers. The motel room already felt emptier. He'd gone from a loner to a person who needed people. He supposed it was healthy, but he didn't look forward to trying to find his balance yet again.

When he woke in the morning, Sam had gone. Blue rolled out of bed and scrubbed his face with his hands. There were people in the motel all around him in the same boat, displaced from their lives, uncertain of the future. Self-pity was a waste of energy.

CPSIA information can be obtained
at www.ICGtesting.com
Printed in the USA
LVHW050501120623
749401LV00002B/160

9 781989 092323